SISKIYOU TRAIL

ALSO BY B.N. RUNDELL

Rindin' Lonesome

Star Dancer

The Christmas Bear

Buckskin Chronicles

McCain Chronicles

Plainsman Western Series

Rocky Mountain Saint Series

Stonecroft Saga

SISKIYOU TRAIL

MCCAIN CRONICLES
BOOK FIVE

B.N. RUNDELL

WOLFPACK
PUBLISHING
— EST 2013 —

Siskiyou Trail
Paperback Edition
Copyright © 2023 B.N. Rundell

Wolfpack Publishing
9850 S. Maryland Parkway, Suite A-5 #323
Las Vegas, Nevada 89183

wolfpackpublishing.com

Paperback ISBN 978-1-63977-847-8
eBook ISBN 978-1-63977-148-6
LCCN 2023945303

DEDICATION

To the sunrise! My favorite time of day, each display of God's brilliance as He splashes color across the sky and dips the bellies of the morning clouds in the molten gold and adds sprinkles of colors across the tops, tells me that God in his grace has given each of us the gift of another day. Undeserving though I may be, His gifts are not dependent on my goodness, but on His grace. And each breath I breathe should be used to tell of His glory and love. Kind of humbling, isn't it? But with each new day, I am reminded that every moment should be treated as the rare commodity that it is—and so I write. Not just to sell books or to please you, the readers, but to use the time He has given in the best and most productive way possible. So, I dedicate this missive to the new day, the sparkling jewel of God's grace and love. Thank you to each of you that has taken this moment of this new day to share with me, you are appreciated.

SISKIYOU TRAIL

CHAPTER 1

COLUMBIA

A bullet whipped past his head, followed by the roar of a big-bore rifle. The thick timber allowed nothing to be seen, but Elijah McCain snatched the Winchester Yellowboy rifle from the scabbard under his right leg and bailed off his big claybank stallion to find cover. Another blast from beyond the woods cut through the trees, followed instantly by a chorus of shouted curses and threats. Two shots stumbled over each other, but both were from lesser weapons —sounding more like pistol shots—and they too, elicited shouts and curses. Eli had dropped into a crouch behind a towering spruce, whose top pierced the blue sky and limbs hung humbly down as if the giant of the forest was doing a curtsy.

Eli moved like the whisper of the morning breeze through the thick woods, each step hushed by the thick carpet of pine needles. As he moved, he searched the woods cautiously, mindful of branches and undergrowth that would sound a warning of his approach as it brushed against his britches. Another shot came from slightly to his left, and another further away. When the big rifle blasted, it was to his right, and the powder smoke lanced from above a thicket of scrub oak under-brush. A clearing showed evidence of a camp, a thin tendril of smoke rose from a fire ring that held nothing but black and grey ashes, packs were stacked on the far side, and the smell of cooked meat mingled with the bitter stench of gunsmoke that lay in the air.

Mumbles came from Eli's left, random words told of at least two angry men plotting their next move, until another big blast came from the brush and the impact of a bullet followed by a grunt and a curse, "That...ol' goat...got me!"

The big rifle boomed again, and the trees belched a man from Eli's left that charged toward the brush, firing his pistol and screaming and shouting profanities. Two mules crashed through the brush, a lone figure rose from behind the scrub oak, fidgeting with a rifle as it looked at the charging shooter with fear-filled wide eyes. The pistol-packing varmint stopped, holding the pistol before him, pointed at his target, and growled, "I gotchu now! I'm gonna enjoy killin' you! You kilt muh partner an' I'm gonna kill you, slow like, so I can watch you die!" He lifted his pistol like it was a hatchet, cocking the hammer as his hand lifted, but the roar of a rifle from the trees sent death riding a lead bullet that pierced his side below the uplifted arm, and bore through his chest to exit out the far side, carrying a big chunk of flesh and a stream of blood with it. The man's knees buckled, and he folded like a dropped deck of well-used cards.

The scraggly-looking figure that had scrambled from the brush, the big rifle held in fumbling fingers, turned to look as Eli walked from the trees, looking about for any other actors from the drama of life and death that had unfolded before him.

"Who're you?" came a voice that was a mix of growls and squeals. Standing before him was a tawdry figure in layers of rags that were at one time long past fine clothes. Thin wisps of grey hair tried to escape the holey hat that was crammed down with a pinned-up front brim atop the mess. Piercing brown eyes, thin eyebrows, wrinkly sun-browned skin, and a grinning mouth that had two teeth, told of a long-time tenant of the woods.

The denizen of the dust started to lift the big bore rifle until Eli spoke, "Whoa now, I'm not one of them. That was my bullet that dropped that last 'un, your cannon took the first one!"

"Wal, who invited you to this hyar party?" retorted the rubble wearing dusty clothes.

"Well, I was travelin' peaceable like and quiet until one of your cannonballs ripped through the trees and almost unseated me from my horse. Although I didn't see my name on the lead, when it whistled past my head I considered that a personal invitation. And to answer your first question, my name is Elijah McCain."

"I'm Beatrice Sinclair," she answered, "An if'n you're hungry, step down, I was 'bout to fix me some fresh caught trout fer muh dinner, got plenty if'n youse of a mind!"

Eli's brow furrowed as his eyes squinted to take a closer look at his new acquaintance. There was little to reveal this was a woman. She wore tattered canvas britches, two or three layers of shirts, a loose hanging jacket that had been mended several times but was in need of more attention, and the colors of the clothes were hidden beneath dirt and grime that spoke of years in the mountains. Movement in the trees behind her caught Eli's attention and he watched as a lop-eared mule pushed from the brush, nudging the woman with its nose and almost toppling her.

"Mabel! Cut that out! Go'on now, get Felix, an' the two of you leave me alone till after muh eatin's done!" Beatrice had turned to swat at the mule as she spewed her demands. She turned to look at Eli, "You stayin' or goin'?"

"I'll fetch my horses," answered Eli, noncommittal as to sharing the meal. He shook his head, chuckling to himself, as he turned away and started into the trees. He had been traveling the freighters' road that sided the Columbia River as the big waters crashed through the Cascades gorge. They were now on the road that led to Fort Raines, one of several blockhouses that had housed troops to protect the portage road from the Cascades. He was bound for Portland, Vancouver, and points beyond as he continued his search for his twin stepsons, Jubal and Joshua Paine, deserters from the Union army who had left home bound for the west and what they thought would be a life of adventure. But the death of their mother, still unknown to them, and a deathbed promise put Eli on their trail to try to get them to return home.

His long-legged stallion Rusty, a lineback red-dun, often called a claybank, was ground tied and grazing contentedly on some patches of grass that sought filtered sunlight through the thick canopy of the forest of towering spruce, fir, and pine. Beside Rusty grazed Grey, the dapple grey mustang pack horse that was laden with two panniers, parfleches, and extra weapons, including a Spencer rifle and a Colt revolver shotgun. The grey and claybank were inseparable trail partners and Eli seldom had to use a lead line to trail the packhorse, letting him travel free rein.

When he returned to the clearing, Beatrice had the fire going and four nice trout skewered and hanging over the little flames. She sat a coffee pot on the rock beside the fire and looked up to Eli, "Have a sit!" motioning to the log on the far side of the fire. "Dinner'll be ready in a jiffy. Got some 'taters in the coals thar," motioning to the fire with a willow stick she used to tend to the trout and more, "If'n you got a cup, coffee'll be ready right soon!"

As Eli seated himself, coffee cup in hand, he looked around the clearing and saw no evidence of the camp being recently used as so many were, but in the few moments he was gone she had settled in well. She cocked her head to the side as she looked at him with a critical eye, scooted closer to the fire and looked at Eli, "What brings you into my neck o' the woods, pilgrim?"

Eli cast a glance to the woman, looked about the area and replied, "You sayin' these are your woods?"

She grinned her toothless grin, cackled with a laugh that shook her whole body and answered, "Tha's right! These're my woods," waving her arm about. "Been abidin' hyar for many years now, so I claim 'em as muh own. That gives me the right to ask all the questions! So, answer me, pilgrim!"

Eli chuckled, "I'm just passin' through on my way downriver, headin' to the mouth of the Columbia." He paused, looking about, and noticed she had already pulled the body of the scoundrel into the bushes, "What was that all about?" he asked, nodding to the booted feet that protruded from under the brush, "Why were they comin' after you? Pardon me for sayin' it, but you don't appear to be a likely candidate for robbing."

She grinned as she cackled, "That's the idea! Don't wanna give nobody the idea I was a rich widow lady an' helpless in the woods. But to answer yore question, not that I need to, mind you, they was after muh gold!"

Eli cocked one eyebrow high as he looked at the woman, "gold?"

"Now, don' you go gettin' no ideas!" she threatened, continuing, "tha's right, gold. Got me quite a bit, but got it hid back yonder a ways. Don't carry no more'n two, three pouches wit' me, just 'nuff fer supplies, you know." She paused, grinning at Eli, "Why wasn't you thinkin' they was after muh body? After all, I'se a good-lookin' woman! I just hide muhself under all this," she motioned to her haggard clothing. She grinned, looking down at herself, "I know Gertrude an' Gloria ain't as perky as they once was," hefting her bosom and cackling, "but under all this, I'm still the good looker whut caught the eyes o' most o' the men that came into the Acey Ducey!"

"I see," replied Eli, stifling his laughter, "I'm surprised you don't have more men chasing after you, and don't worry, I don't have any interest in any gold, yours or anyone's. I'm only interested in finding my boys." He let the last statement drop off into almost a whisper as he looked to the trees to see the big mule push through the woods, followed by a second, almost identical mule.

CHAPTER 2

PORTAGE

The fog lay heavy on the water of the Columbia River, its feathery vapors lifting into the thick forest that rode the shoulders and ridges that sided the Columbia River Gorge. The narrow game trail Eli followed through the thick woods kept him away from the road used by the freighters and others involved in the portage of the Cascades. Most shippers preferred their cargo to be portaged to another steamboat to make the rest of the journey either way, whether east to Walla Walla or the Snake River to make its way to the Montana Territory gold fields, or if west bound, to the cities of Portland, Vancouver, or even points west to the mouth of the Columbia. Although he planned to stop in the cities and ask around, Eli was more comfortable traveling in the thick woods, keeping away from other travelers and mischief makers.

Occasionally, a break in the timber afforded him a view of the deep canyon below or across the river to the south bank and the mountains beyond. It was mid-afternoon when just such a break caught his attention and he stopped, leaning on the pommel of his saddle, and with arms crossed on the saddle horn, he took in the view on the far bank. A sliver of silver cascaded over the face of a tall cliff, dropping what he guessed to be five or six hundred feet, with rocky shoulders and tall timber on either side, he marveled in the beauty of God's handiwork. Below the falls he saw the narrow stream drop over the edge of the gorge and plummet into the river below. It was not his first sighting of waterfalls on either side of the river, but that had to be the most spectacular. He lifted his eyes to the distance and saw a lone sentinel with his white hood standing guard over the entire region. The tall mountain with its hoary head must be Mount Hood. He grinned, looked heavenward and said quietly, "That's beautiful, God," a sentiment he often expressed on his travels through the mountains.

As he continued he passed a point that he reckoned to be Cape Horn, a landing used by riverboats and more. Although he had never been in this area, Eli always made it a habit to talk to other travelers and capture every description, name of landmarks, trails, and more so that he had a mental map of the land he would travel. Because of the basaltic cliffs below the trail, and the prominent rock in the middle of the river that stood over eighty feet high and at least a hundred yards around the base, he knew this to be Cape Horn, and when he crossed a small stream and heard the crashing of waters below, he knew that to be the Cape Horn falls.

He bent down to stroke the neck of his big stallion, "Rusty, not too much further to go and we should come to a settlement some are calling Washougally Camp, others call it Parkersville, but from what I'm told, it's just a settlement of farms, not much else. We'll be makin' camp soon, big boy," he sat upright, twisted around to look at the grey packhorse and saw the black wolf pup, Lobo, who had adopted him and the horses as his family and was now crowding a hundred pounds of canine muscle, but he stayed with them and had become Eli's friend and foot warmer when they slept. Eli applied a little knee pressure and nudged his mount onward, followed closely by the pack horse, and a black streak slashed through the trees to his right as Lobo passed the horses and took his place at the head of the entourage to scout the trail before them.

When he broke from the woods, the land opened to a wide flats that showed early settlers with cabins and more as they established bountiful farms. The sun was tucking itself below the western horizon, but there was still light aplenty, and he pushed on, pointing Rusty to the road closer to the river. Eli spotted a riverboat at a wharf and several wagons nearby, his curiosity pushed him on, and he was soon beside a farmer's loaded wagon, "Greetings friend, could you tell me if this is Washougally Camp?"

The man turned to look skeptically at the stranger who sat on a tall red-dun horse, and answered, "It's been called that, and Parkersville, but most of us hereabouts call it Washougal."

Eli looked at the loaded wagon, "This appears to be fine farm land, and I see you've had a good crop of corn and more. Shipping it west?"

"That's right, lotta them gold diggers get hungry for fresh vegetables, and they pay dearly. Makes for a good return on the year's work."

As they spoke, the many farmers crowded nearer the boat and wasted little time getting their goods unloaded and a bill of lading from the captain. In just a few minutes, the farmer that spoke with Eli got his wagon unloaded, and he and his helper stepped down. Barked orders and directions came from a burly roustabout and by the way he was ordering the crew around, Eli took him to be the first mate. Showing little regard to both crew and shippers alike, he seemed to relish ordering others around. Eli was biding his time until the captain was free, but he caught the eye of the mate and was suddenly the subject of his wrath.

"You there! Git on away from here, you lazy lout! Can't you see we got workin' men here? Quit botherin' them farmers and git on yore way, y'hear?" As he spoke, he strutted through the stacked goods and made his way closer to Eli.

Eli looked about, unsure whether he was the subject of the mate's derision, but a quick look his way saw the man swaggering toward him, shaking his fist in the air as he shouted his orders and was glaring his way. Eli grimaced, swung a leg over the cantle of his saddle and stepped to the ground, moving away from Rusty. The blowhard tried to bull up, pushing out his chest and stomping his way nearer. In a calm voice, Eli asked, "So, what's got you so all-fired mad?" and gave no ground to the man.

The mate stepped in front of Eli, put fists on his hips, "You got no bizness hyar, git on your way!" he demanded as he waved an arm toward the woods.

"First off, it's of no concern to you whether I have business or not, and besides that, you have no authority once you step off that boat!" responded Eli, still keeping his voice calm and showing a hint of mischief in his grin. He had crossed his arms over his chest, stood with legs spread, and an unobtrusive hand lingering over the butt of the Colt pistol holstered at his hip.

The mate glared, gritting his teeth, flexing the

muscles in his jaw as his hands came off his hips. Eli's experience bode him well as he watched the man ready his bull charge. As soon as the mate moved his foot to begin his lunge, Eli dropped his hands to his side, palms open and dropped into a crouch. The mate swung his arms wide, lowered his head, and lunged, expecting to wrap Eli in his wide arms and crush him in a bear hug. But Eli made a quick step to his left, slapped the Mate's right arm down as Eli bent his knee forward and tripped the man over his knee, grabbing his shoulder and driving him into the ground face first.

Spitting dirt, the mate rolled to his side and clambered to his feet, growling and glaring. He prided himself on a rough-and-tumble, no-holds-barred way of fighting and he had never taken a fall like he just experienced. In a crouch, arms outstretched, he began to circle a grinning Eli, who casually moved to the side, arms loosely at his side, "You sure you want to do this?" he asked, warily watching the mate, but Eli knew this man was aware that his entire crew had stopped to watch, several mounting the second deck and standing at the rail. With a glance to the boat, the mate charged, growling as he came. Eli feinted another step to the left, but stayed where he stood and met the charge with a flurry of fists to the man's face until he straightened up and Eli continued the barrage to his mid-section. The mate tried to block the blows, but Eli kept them coming, and the man began to wilt as he back-stepped to escape. Eli gave way and let the man move back, catch his breath and flex his fists, glaring at Eli.

Again, Eli grinned, cocked his head to the side, and said, "There's no shame in quitting now," he offered, but the man growled and came at Eli. He bobbed and weaved, but Eli was not to be fooled, for he had been trained well by a champion fighter and was well experienced. A big powerhouse right came whistling as a roundhouse blow, but Eli turned away and caught the glancing blow on the side of his head. Eli staggered back and the mate pressed his charge with a left-handed jab, but Eli ducked away, bringing his fist from the ground and burying it in the mate's gut. A grunt was forced from the mate as he doubled over, only to catch an uppercut that smashed his nose across his face, splattering blood everywhere.

The mate staggered, back peddled, his foot turning on a stone, and fell flat on his back, knocking the air from his lungs. He struggled to breathe, flopping his arms away from his chest, he rolled to his side to crawl and come to his feet. He shook his head, growled, "I'm gonna kill you for that!" and started toward Eli, but held his fists up to guard his face and the expected onslaught from Eli.

With a chuckle and a grin, Eli moved side to side, feinted with a left jab and followed it with a roundhouse head banger, staggering the mate back on his heels, but he quickly caught himself, and with head down, came in swinging. Eli met him with a stabbing jab that flattened the pulp of his nose, smashed his lip against his teeth and broke off one of his teeth. The mate's head rocked back, and Eli came with head down, fists pumping as he crashed into the man, the flurry of fists finding the mate's belly and ribs.

The mate pushed Eli back, struggled to catch his wind, and looked at Eli with frightened eyes. Eli grinned, began moving around the mate, side-stepping and bobbing and weaving, avoiding the weak attempts at boxing by the mate. Suddenly the mate dropped his hands slightly, feinted a charge and stepped quickly to the side, following his lunge with a wide, looping, hard right fist that crashed against Eli's head and staggered him back on his heels.

Darkness clouded his vision and Eli felt himself falling but his hands did not move, and he crashed on his back, losing his wind. He covered his face, rubbing his eyes, trying to see and heard the man roar as he charged. Eli knew what to expect and lifted his knees just as the man lunged, arms outstretched, expecting to crush Eli with his full weight, but even with blurred vision, Eli brought up his knees, caught the weight of the man as he lunged, and flipped him over his head to crash on his back with a dust raising thud.

Eli rolled away quickly, pushed himself off the ground and shook his head as he looked through squinted eyes and blurred vision, but he saw no movement from the form on the ground. Eli bent at the waist, hands on his knees, breathing heavily, and looked at the mate squirming on his back. Eli straightened, blinked and shook his head, his vision began to clear, and he saw the mate coming to his feet. With another roar, the mate charged, but Eli surprised him as he stepped into the charge, turned his hip toward the man and caught him, wrapping an arm around his shoulder and with a twist and a shove, Eli threw the mate with a hip roll and dropped him on his side. He followed the man to the ground, drove his knee into the mate's side, and pushed him face down. With one knee in the middle of the mate's back, Eli grabbed a handful of hair and bent his head back, stretching his neck as Eli put his mouth beside the man's ear and spoke softly and calmly, "It's time to quit this nonsense. I don't have anything against you, and you don't even know me. Are you ready to call it quits?"

The mate grunted, struggling to breathe, and tried to nod. Eli loosened his grip, and the mate said, "We're done."

"Good," replied Eli. He loosed his grip on the mate, came to his feet and stepped back. As the man rolled to his back, Eli offered him a hand and the mate accepted, came to his feet, shaking his head, bent over, hands on knees, and mumbled, "Ain't never been beat like that b'fore!" He looked up at Eli, extended his hand and the two shook hands, nodded, and turned away, the mate to his boat and Eli to his horses.

CHAPTER 3

PORTLAND

Eli went to the river's edge to splash some water on his face and hands and let the horses have a drink. The stretch of his legs felt good and as he stood beside Rusty, a voice came from behind him, "I been wantin' to see that for some time now."

Eli turned to see the captain of the moored steamship. He turned and extended his hand to shake, "Captain. I'm Elijah McCain. Sorry 'bout that, I didn't expect to be jumped like that and, well…" he shrugged.

"And I'm Captain John Wolf of the Wilson G. Hunt steamer. And there's no need for any apology. You have my thanks and probably that of most of the crew as well. That man, Ryder, has been bullying his way over every crew member, passenger, freighters, and more, for I don't know how long. Every time I get after him, he makes promises he has no intention of keeping, believing his position as first mate and his willingness to fight will get him his way every time, and so far, it has."

"Why don't you get rid of him?" asked Eli, frowning, as the two men walked back to the stacked freight.

"His daddy's J. W. Ruckle, one of the founders of the Oregon Steam Navigation Company, owners of this boat. Daddy can't handle him either, and he put him on this boat to get him out of his hair, and 'tween you 'n me, I think he was thinkin' that this boat had seen better days and was about due for a boiler blow or something that would solve his headaches with his son!"

"Are you headed upriver or down?" asked Eli.

"Up. Most of this," waving his hand at the stacked goods, "is bound for the goldfields. We'll pick up more from the portage to take back downriver. And so it goes..." He grinned at Eli, turned to sit on one of the crates. He motioned to Eli to join him, waving to another crate just opposite.

As he seated himself, Eli dug out his always-present tintype and handed it to the captain, "Those are my twin sons, Jubal and Joshua. I heard they worked on your boat for a while recently and I've been lookin' for 'em." He nodded to the tintype in the captain's hands, "They look familiar to you?"

The captain frowned, glanced from the tintype to Eli and back. "Don't recall anyone by the name of McCain," he drawled, passing the tintype back to Eli.

"Their name is Paine, they're my stepsons. Before she died, their mother asked me to find them and get them to come home. They don't know about their mother and had left home before she took ill. They were in the Union army and because I was a career soldier, they probably think I'm huntin' 'em because they deserted, but that's of no concern to me now. I just want to find them to keep the promise I made their mother."

The captain grinned, "I know about promises to wives, yessir. And to answer your question, yes, they were on our boat from the cascades to Vancouver. We had a lay-over for a couple days and the entire crew covered Vancouver and Portland 'fore we headed out and went downriver to Monticello and on to Astoria. I talked with your boys at some length and I think they were just on a grand adventure, you know, boys wanting to see what's on the other side of the mountain. They had quite a few questions about the sailing ships, seems they had some family connection to them, and asked about sailing and the life at sea." He chuckled, nodding to the Hunt, "Even that ol' boat came 'round the horn before she made it up here to gold country." He chuckled again, "They were kind of surprised to learn that several paddle wheelers took to sea to come around the horn."

"And they didn't come back upriver with you?" asked Eli.

"No, they were last seen in a grog shop in Astoria, talkin' to some of the crew from one of the sailing ships. They sent word they were not coming back aboard, so we headed back upriver, loaded with smoked salmon and more."

Eli sighed heavily, "Remember anything that might help in my search? The name of the grog shop, any ship names, anything that might help?"

"The grog shop was called the Red Rooster. Other'n that, don't know of anything else. Astoria's a busy port, ship's comin' an' goin' all the time." He paused, looking at Eli, "I don't envy you your search, but I hope you find 'em. They're good boys."

"Thanks captain. That seems to be the story of my search...too little, too late. But, I've got a promise to keep, so I best be movin' on." Eli stood, extended his hand to shake, "Thanks again, captain. It's always good to at least hear about the boys, know they're doin' alright."

The captain stood, shook hands with Eli and added, "I'll keep 'em in my prayers, an' you too!"

"Need all the prayers we can get, and I'll do the same for you and your crew."

The captain chuckled, "You already answered one of 'em, what with the whippin' you gave the first mate."

Eli grinned as he reached for the rein of Rusty, stepped into the stirrup and swung aboard.

———

ELI SAT AT THE TABLE, newspaper in hand, as he savored the last of his morning coffee. He had taken a ferry across the Columbia River to take a room in the log cabin hotel in Portland and spend the night refreshing himself with a bath, the night in a bed, and breakfast in the café. He had downed his eggs, bacon, and biscuits with gravy and now sat before his third cup of coffee. He read where the recent storms had taken down the telegraph line to Vancouver and the line that stretched across the Willamette had also been downed. The page advertising businesses boasted about the carriages and concord wagons manufactured by the F.A. Hake company, and the Portland Foundry and Machine Shop advertised their steam engines.

Although Portland had its own paper, this copy of the State Rights Democrat from Albany had apparently been left behind by a previous coffee drinker. He perused an article by the Rev. H.H. Spaulding that spoke of Lincoln's assassination and the apostate condition of the nation, then folded the paper and lay it aside as he picked up his coffee and looked out the window to the awakening business on the main street of Portland. A soft voice behind him asked, "More coffee, sir?"

Eli turned to see a young woman with a frilly apron covering her front and a smile with sparkling blue eyes that lit up the room as she stood holding the big coffee pot. It appeared too heavy for her as she grasped the handle with one hand and held the base with a heavy pot-holder underneath in her other hand. Eli nodded, "Please," and moved the cup closer to her.

As she poured the coffee she asked, "New to the area are you sir?"

"Yes'm. Just passing through, headed to Astoria."

She filled the cup, stepped back and smiled, "Astoria? That gentleman there," nodding to a trapper-looking, whiskery-faced man in buckskins, "just came from there."

"That's good to know. Thank you, miss."

"You're quite welcome, sir. Enjoy your stay in our town."

Eli finished his coffee and walked to the table where the buckskinner was finishing his breakfast and enjoying his second cup of coffee. "Excuse me, sir, but the wait-ress said you just came in from Astoria, is that right?"

The man finished his coffee, sat the cup down and looked up at Eli, one eyebrow cocked high as he gave him the once-over. "Yeah, so?" he grumbled.

Nothing about his expression said welcome nor any threat, but Eli continued, "I'm headin' up that way, it's new country to me and I'd like to learn a little about it, if you have the time."

"How ya' goin'?" grumbled the buckskinner.

"Horseback, prefer the game trails and such."

The man let a slow grin split his whiskers, nodded for Eli to be seated, and waved the waitress over for some more coffee. When both cups were filled, the buck-skinner spoke, "I'm Patches, you're?"

"Eli McCain. Been following a couple men, my sons, from St. Louis, through Montana territory, Washington, and now headed to Astoria."

"Why you goin' to Astoria?"

"Got word from over at the Red Rooster that my boys had jumped on another steamer and headed downriver to Astoria. They were with a couple men that had been on a tall ship as deck hands and the four of 'em were said to be goin' to Astoria to get aboard as crew of a tall ship."

"They in trouble?" asked the burly man.

"No, their mother asked me to try to get them to go home and take over the family farm. They joined the Union Army, deserted, headed west. Been followin' 'em but haven't caught up with 'em yet."

"Unnerstan', ain't easy findin' a soul in these hyar thick woods. Been workin' 'em fer nigh unto a decade an' ain't seen 'em all yet." He paused for some more coffee, looked at Eli, "You 'pear to be a sojer boy your own self. Was ya?"

"I was. Wore the blue for most of nineteen years, not counting West Point. Stationed at Fort Laramie, spent considerable time in the west, fell in love with the mountains."

"Yup. I started trappin' in the Rockies, but the market fer beaver never came back. Scouted some fer the army, led a couple wagon trains crost' the rockies an' into the Willamette valley. Last time, decided to stay." Another sip of steaming coffee allowed a brief respite, but Patches continued, "Best way to get back yonder to Astoria is the upper end o' what some're callin' the Columbia River Trail. It sides the west bank most o' the way. Easy trail, but if'n you like the thicker woods, there's game trails back in the deeper parts. I been thinkin' 'bout headin' up north muh ownself, might see fit to show you the way, if'n you was to ask me real nice." He chuckled as he lifted the cup to savor the aroma as well as the taste of the coffee.

Eli grinned, liking the cut of the man, and replied, "Gotta get re-supplied, pull out at first light. Suit you?"

"It do. I'm holed up down to the livery where you got your horses. That is yore big red dun, ain't it?"

Eli chuckled, "It is. First light then?"

"I'll be ready."

CHAPTER 4

TRAIL

The reflection of the first grey light bounced off the ripples of the Columbia River as the two men rode the trail that lay at the edge of the towering spruce and pine. The ancient trail had become what most considered to be a wagon road, made so by the many settlers that had traveled the Oregon Trail from the eastern states, anxious to find the choice locations in the fertile lands west of the Willamette River. Elijah McCain and Patches, new friends, were bound for the northernmost point of Oregon, where lay the port city of Astoria, hopeful of finding Eli's boys, or at least some word of their travels.

The two men traveled side-by-side and Patches prided himself in his knowledge of the country and was enjoying sharing his knowledge with Eli. The sun was rising just off and behind their right shoulder, the brightness of early morning warming their backs. "That yonder," began Patches, pointing before them, "is what they call Sauvie Island, land of the Multnomah people, part of the Chinookan peoples. Ain't too many of 'em left, most been sent to the Grande Ronde reservation, but they come back when the salmon're runnin'! Peaceable folks, mostly. Good people."

Patches twisted in his saddle, elbow on the pommel, "This hyar venture will take us nigh unto three, mebbe four days, less'n you got other plans. Do ya?"

Eli chuckled, knowing this was the first time that Patches had slowed his verbal assault to listen. "No, no other plans."

"That suits."

"Any other Native peoples in this part of the country?"

Patches looked at Eli, "Why, you fearful of 'em?"

Eli chuckled, "No, but I am curious and if there are any that are prone to mischief makin', I'd like to be prepared."

Patches huffed, shaking his head, "Should allus be prepared anyhow! An' to answer yore question, there's the Clackamas people, they ain't so many no more. They been sent to the same reservation wit' the Multomah. The Clackamas was known for their fishin', they used dip nets to take the salmon durin' the run. Made themselves wood platforms that hung o'er the water, dipped their nets and brought 'em up full. They traded the fish to other tribes an' the white man fer what're they needed. Did purty well till they accepted the treaty 'bout a decade ago. They, like some others, practiced head flattenin', you know, tyin' boards on the little 'uns heads, flattened their foreheads, that was 'posed to show they was free people, not slaves."

Eli shook his head, frowned, looking around at the flats to his right where the big island showed no resemblance to an island, but more like a common bottom land farm country. There were scattered houses and barns, tall cornstalks with silk showing it was ready for harvest, waves of grain fields moving in the morning breeze, some fields showing farmers with wagons cutting their crops, overall, a very tranquil scene. To their left, low-rising slopes were barren of timber yet showed fields of stumps where the timber had been taken for homes and more. The scars of civilization were everywhere, from the widening of trails for wagons, to the plowing and planting of fields for farms, and Eli shook his head at the destruction of God's creation at the hands of mankind.

Patches had been watching Eli and his reaction to the clearing of the land, with a stoic expression, he spoke, "Sickenin' ain't it?"

Eli frowned as he looked at his new friend, "What?"

Patches waved his arm in a wide arc to take in most of what they viewed, "I'm tellin' ya, it's plumb sickenin'! All them farmers an' such clearing the land, cuttin' down trees that've been here for hunnerts o' years just so's they can put a roof o'er their heads to block out them wunnerful stars God hung up yonder." He paused, looking about, "Just don' seem right, it don' at all, nosiree!"

THE TERRAIN of western Oregon was low rolling hills with a few round-topped buttes interspersed with the random high-rising snow-capped peaks that rode the Cascades like Mt. Hood, the Sisters and Broken Top, and more. But the northernmost arm of western Oregon prided itself more on the thick timber rather than mountain peaks. The Western red cedar, Douglas fir, Western hemlock and others grew in close proximity to many more, making the thick dark forests seem impenetrable, but this is where the game trail followed by Eli and Patches offered the two travelers anonymity and cover.

Their trail had hugged the tree line at the base of rolling hills until the timber stretched fingers of pines toward the Columbia. The two men kept to the trail that bent into the thick timber and rode the shoulder of a low-rising hill until it dropped off the north end and crossed a wagon road before climbing the crest of a timbered butte that appeared to be the highest point around. It was near the crest that Eli suggested they make camp for the night, "We've covered a bit of ground today, and I'm gettin' a mite hungry. Reckon we oughta make camp, what say?"

Patches chuckled, "I been waitin' fer you to say sumpin'. Muh horse has been lookin' at me like I was mistreatin' him. If'n you start makin' camp, I'll see if'n I can get us one o' them turkeys we saw back yonder."

"Turkey sounds good. That li'l pool below the spring yonder will give us enough water for the horses and the coffee pot, so, I'll get things started while you go huntin'," suggested Eli.

Patches grinned, chuckled, "Yore already soundin' like a wife, but I'll do it."

They stripped the horses, gave them a rubdown with some dry grass, picketed them and began their separate duties. As Patches started out, he checked his rifle, chuckled as he looked at Eli, "Muh hearin' ain't what it used to be, but I still can call them turkeys in to dinner good 'nuff!" He chuckled again as he disappeared into the trees. Eli scooped up a pot full of spring water for their coffee and soon had a small fire going. He sat down on his outstretched bedroll in the shade of a big hemlock and had just leaned back to watch the coffee pot begin its dance when he heard the muffled report of a gunshot. He grinned, thinking Patches had bagged them a turkey and he pulled his hat down on his eyes and relaxed.

Lobo nudged Eli, trying to wake him, his cold nose on his cheek. Eli grunted, frowned, then came immediately awake, but as was his usual caution, he slowly opened his eyes and looked under the brim of his hat to see what had disturbed the wolf. Lobo had slipped away into the trees and that was a sure sign something was amiss, and they might have visitors. Eli heard the crunch of gravel and the whisper of pine branches on clothing. He thought it might be Patches, but he would have announced himself. Eli knew it was not Natives so it must be white men that were coming closer without calling out. His arms were crossed on his chest and his right hand rested on the butt of his Colt as he started to stir. He used his left hand to push up his hat and yawned and sat up, looking about.

"Hold it right there! Don't go movin' less'n you want to get the same thing yore partner got!" growled a voice from the trees beyond the fire. The voice lowered as he spoke to another man with him, "Get his gun Willy!"

Eli saw a man somewhat attired like a deck hand of a ship with long-sleeved knit shirt, duck pants and deck shoes who started toward Eli. He stepped between Eli and the talker, giving Eli the chance to drag his Colt and come to his feet. He grabbed the one known as Willy, jerked him close with his arm around his neck, stepped behind him and held the pistol at Willy's ear and barked to the other man, "Drop it!" he demanded, watching the man who stood at a crouch at the edge of the trees holding a rifle at his hip but aimed at Eli.

"Hah! You think I care what'chu do to him? Go 'head, choot him! Then I'll drop you where you stand!" demanded the intruder. He started to lift his rifle to bring the muzzle to bear but Eli pushed Willy aside and fired. The Colt barked, bucked, and spat lead and smoke, startling the rifleman, but the real surprise showed on his face as the bullet blossomed red on his chest, pushing him back a step and causing him to drop the rifle. Eli cocked the pistol again, but the man sat down, stared at his chest, looked up at Eli, "You kilt me!" he mumbled and with one last ragged breath, dropped his chin to his chest, his eyes staring sightlessly at his ragged britches.

Eli turned the pistol on Willy, "Stay right where you are! Now, what'd you do with Patches, the buckskinner?"

"Hank shot him! We was follerin' yore tracks when Hank heard a turkey, but it were yore frien', and we jumped behin' some trees, we was hid real good, an' when that feller showed he gobbled like a turkey an' Hank shot him!"

"No warning, nothing? Just shot him?"

"Uuhuh, yup, that's what Hank done. That feller weren't 'spectin' no turkey with a gun!" He cackled at his own wit, looked up at Eli, lifted his hands, "Not me! I din't do it! Hank done it! I din't e'en have a gun!" he whined.

Eli motioned with his pistol, "Take me to him, go ahead, lead the way!" demanded Eli, stepping closer as Willy scrambled to his feet. They pushed through the trees, moving downslope from the crest and following no particular trail. Willy was not a woodsman and made enough noise to alarm any living thing. A slight clearing showed, and the crumpled form of Patches lay in the tall grass, his rifle under his body. Eli motioned Willy away, "Stay right there!" He walked to where Patches lay and went to one knee, rolled Patches to his back to see blank eyes and a blood-soaked chest. The bullet had taken him high in his chest, causing him to choke to death on his own blood. Eli shook his head, glanced up to see Willy take off through the trees, crashing his way to escape.

CHAPTER 5

POSSE

It was a restless night for Eli, although he made a pine-bough lean-to for shelter, the short-lived storm paid little heed to the shelter, and it served little purpose for Eli and Lobo. The horses were better protected under the heavy branches of the big spruce, but they stood hipshot and heads down as Eli and Lobo crowded under the big tree with them. Lightning stretched bony fingers through the trees, thunder rumbled and shook the ground, and the rain was merciless, continually seeking out any unprotected creature to drench with its downpour.

Eli guessed it to be about three in the morning when the stars pushed their way through the darkness and the bashful moon made its return. The black clouds kept the lightning in their skirts as the storm retreated to the plains to follow the river's course to the east. The quiet of the night returned with the only sounds those of branches shedding water and thin courses of runoff water making their way off the butte top. The cooing call of mourning doves beckoned the soon rise of the sun, but darkness was slow to relent its grip on the land.

Eli started foraging for any dry wood, mostly dry branches that adorned the lower reaches of the spruce and pine. He soon had a fire going and the coffee pot crowding the fire to warm its water for his morning coffee. He dug out the frying pan and some bacon to begin his breakfast. With some left-over corn meal biscuits, he was anxious to put some miles behind him.

After his third cup of coffee and the disappearance of all the biscuits and bacon, he reluctantly began rigging the horses. With a last look around, he swung aboard and nudged Rusty to the ancient game trail that cut through the trees, but a hail from the trees stopped him. He dropped his hand to the butt of his Colt and answered, "Who are you and whatdaya want?"

Eli heard horses pushing through the trees before and behind him and backed Rusty to the edge of the trees to allow him to cover both breaks in the trees. The first to show himself came with one hand open and lifted, the other holding the reins high, "Hang on there, friend. I'm Jackson Preacher, sheriff of Columbia County. We're lookin' for a couple outlaws, thought you might be one of 'em." The sheriff pushed further into the clearing, followed closely by another man sporting a tin star. Two men came from Eli's left, also wearing deputy badges and holding their pistols before them.

"Whoa there, boys. Put them pistols away. We don't even know who this man is and if he was one of 'em or not," demanded the sheriff, looking at the two men on the far side of the clearing from him. He looked at Eli, "What's yore name, an' what're you doin' hereabouts?"

"I'm Elijah McCain. I'm headed to Astoria, searching

for my twin sons that were said to have been taken on a ship outta the harbor there."

"Any proof of that?" asked the sheriff, looking from Eli to his posse and back.

"You tell me about the men you're lookin' for, what'd they do and what'd they look like. I might have seen 'em," responded Eli, keeping his hand on the butt of his Colt. He had leaned forward, his left elbow on the pommel, his right hand under the flap of his coat at his left hip.

"Ah, quit palaverin' sheriff! He's prob'ly one of 'em. They said there was two, one with whiskers, the other'n without. They said the big'n did the shootin' an' kilt the teller. He's prob'ly the second one what did the shootin'! Ain't no other reason to be hidin' out up here in the woods! Let's take him or hang him righ'chere!" demanded the man in the lead on Eli's left, waving his pistol around and threatening Eli.

"Hold on, Clarence! We don't know if'n he's one or not!" He looked at Eli, "Why are you here?"

"I told you. Now, about the two men you're lookin' for," began Eli, nodding to the impatient talker, "other than whiskers and not, what'd they look like, how tall, old, you know?"

The sheriff frowned, "Two men, older man had full whiskers, bigger'n me, the other'n was clean shaven, smaller, mousy lookin'."

Eli shook his head, looked at the loudmouth deputy, "And just which one do you think I am?"

"Wal, you could be the big un, shaved yore whiskers off. And wha'chu doin' with that extry horse? Anyhow, you ain't said why yore hidin' out up here!" growled the disgruntled deputy.

Eli nodded to his right, "If you'll check over there

'bout twenty yards, there's some rocks piled up and you'll find the whiskered one there. As far as the other one, he squealed a lot as he ran off last night. I didn't care to chase after him." He paused, added, "And if you'll look down there 'bout fifty yards or so, there's a clearing. At the edge you'll find another grave. That's my partner, Patches." He nodded to the bay on the lead, standing by the grey packhorse, "This is his horse. Your outlaws killed him before they came after me."

The sheriff, still skeptical, squinted at Eli, "How's 'bout you steppin' down while we check out those graves?"

Eli nodded and stepped down as the sheriff ordered two of his deputies to find the graves and report back. He looked directly at the vocal one, "You, Clarence, you find that'n," pointing to the direction indicated by Eli, "and uncover enough so you see his face to be sure."

With a grumble and a snarl, the deputy complied and pushed his mount through the trees with a glare at Eli as he passed. The sheriff also stepped down, ground-tied his mount and walked closer to Eli. He frowned as he asked, "Tell me 'bout your boys."

Eli dug out the tintype, handed it to the sheriff and explained, "I was in the war, career soldier before that, not home much, and the boys grew up without me. They decided to join up, but the war was not for them, and they deserted. They headed west, trying to get away, make their fortune and have a grand adventure. I promised their mother, on her deathbed, that I would try to find them, encourage them to return home and take over her family's farm in Kentucky. They keep movin', I keep followin', I think they know I'm on their trail, but I also think they believe I will turn them in as deserters."

The sheriff looked long and hard at the tintype,

listening to Eli's story, handed it back and asked, "Will you?"

"No, the war's over, but I believe they think me bein' a career soldier, that I would only go by the book and turn them in, but that's all in the past. They don't even know about their mother."

"What outfit were you in, in the war, I mean?"

"Sheridan's Cavalry at the last battle, Appomattox. I commanded a brigade. Mustered out right after that."

"Commanded? What was your rank?"

"Lieutenant Colonel. Graduated West Point in '48, served at Fort Laramie and a few other posts before the war."

"I was a captain with the 5th Cavalry."

Eli frowned, "That was a colored outfit, wasn't it?"

"It was, but not the officers. Most of the non-comms were colored, but the officers were all white."

Eli grinned, "You have a sergeant major?"

"Ummhmm, good man, Moses Carpenter."

Eli grinned, "He and several of his friends are home-steading over by the Yakama reservation. Moses served with me at the last battle of Appomattox."

"You don't say! Well, I'll be dad-gummed if I ever thought I'd see that rascal again. Reckon I'll hafta make it o'er that way some day and look him up!" He shook his head, grinning, looked at Eli, "Small world, ain't it?"

"It is that."

The two dispatched deputies returned, the vocal one a bit long-faced as he looked at the sheriff, "Looks like they said, burly man, whiskers, and stinkin' worse'n any skunk!" he growled, glancing to Eli with a scowl.

Eli grinned, "He didn't smell none too purty 'fore I buried him."

The second deputy reported, "That'n down yonder

had whiskers too, but he was wearin' buckskins and was showin' grey in his hair. Don't think he were one o' them outlaws."

The sheriff nodded at the reports, looked at Eli, "Which way did the other'n run off to?"

Eli nodded to the trail that led down the south side of the butte, "Thataway. He was afoot and runnin' scared. He thought I was gonna shoot him in the back and was screamin', 'don't shoot, don't shoot' as he ran."

The sheriff walked back to his horse, mounted up, looked at his deputies, "Alright men, we'll head off down that way, see if we can pick up any tracks. Course, it'll be a mite difficult what with the rain, but we'll see what we can do." He looked at Eli, "Good luck on your hunt!"

"Thanks, sheriff, you too!" replied Eli as he swung aboard Rusty and grabbed up the leads of the bay and the grey packhorse.

CHAPTER 6

ASTORIA

"Do you know what you see?" came a voice from the shadows of tall spruce and hemlock. Eli had stopped, leaned on the pommel of his saddle with arms crossed to look at the flats between him and the Columbia River. He turned to see an old man, long grey hair hanging past his shoulders, and held back from his face with a narrow headband. His eyes were dark but bright, his face showed a hint of laughter, and his form, though old, was strong. He stepped from the shadows and walked closer, yet turned to face the flats. He pointed to the north, "That is the Columbia River, the marshland before us is called Skunk Cabbage Flats." He paused, looked at Eli, "You have come far?"

"You might say that," and with a glance around, "thinkin' 'bout makin' camp before I go further." Eli shaded his eyes to look further into the distance to the north, "Looks to be some farms out there."

"This was the land of my people, the Tlatskanai, some call us the Clatskanie, but the white people came, and because we were few and did not make war, they thought we were weak and took our lands from us. It was many years ago, before my hair looked like winter's snow."

Eli stepped down, extended his hand to the old man, "My name is Eli. I am not here to take anyone's land, and what happened to you and your people, I believe was wrong, but I have heard many stories like yours. But as you know, good and bad people are found among all peoples."

The old man hesitated, looked at Eli with a critical eye, and extended his hand to shake with Eli, "You have a good heart, Eli. I am called Long Walker, and if you want, I will share my camp with you. I have fresh smoked salmon, but little else."

Eli grinned, "I have coffee, and will make some corn dodgers and we'll have us a fine meal!" He motioned for Long Walker to lead the way and led his horses as he followed the old man.

The old man had added some yampa root, baked them in the coals as the corn dodgers danced in the pan, and the new friends had a bountiful feast in the shadows of the towering trees. Eli asked, "It appears you've been camped here a good spell; don't you have a village?"

Grey hair tumbled over the man's shoulders as he looked up at Eli, "There are few of us left. The only thing the white man gave us was his spotted disease, it took many of my people. Now those that remain are forced to live alone or join with the Klamath. I am Tlatskanai and I will always be Tlatskanai. Even when the white men take all the salmon in the river, I will still be Tlatskanai, and I will die as one. The white men have even taken the name of my people and put it on the river," motioning with his head to the stream below the camp, "and their village which lies in the valley."

"You say they're taking all the salmon?" asked Eli, frowning, as he sipped the last of his coffee.

Long Walker pointed to the Columbia in the distance beyond the flats, "There! They have put their building on the trees they call pilings in the river. They put long nets across the waters to take the fish and in the building, they put the meat into containers, dump the remains in the water. They say the cases will go far away to feed more people." He looked down at the dregs in his cup, tossed them aside and held his cup for more coffee, watched as Eli filled it, and continued. "If other people want fish, they should come get their own."

Eli dropped his eyes, remembering the news of the Donation Land Claim Act of 1850 that allowed white settlers to lay claim to 320-acre parcels of land in the Oregon Territory and married couples could get twice that, all by coming into the Oregon Territory and staking their claim. It was that act that prompted so many families to take to the Oregon Trail and move west to claim their share of free land. Most did so without any regard or concern for the Native peoples that lived on the land and consequently, the Natives fought back, and the Indian Wars spread across the west. After the war, the Homestead Acts added more fuel to the fire of settlers versus the Natives. It was not just a matter of white men getting their own fish, it was much more.

"And you, Long Walker, are you going to spend the rest of your days here," looking around at the towering trees, "in the woods, all alone?"

"I am not alone. The spirits of my people are always with me." He lifted his hands to the trees and the fading light of the sky, "this is my land. This is my home. I will always be here, and when my spirit leaves my body, I will still be here."

Eli sat silent, considering the man and his thoughts, knowing that every man wants to believe that he will live forever, whether in this life or the next. But even though the thought might give comfort in the sunset years, unless one has the assurance of more than simple thought, can there be any true comfort? Eli remembered the words of Scripture and thought of John 3:18 *He that believeth on Him is not condemned: but he that believeth not is condemned already, because he hath not believed in the name of the only begotten Son of God.*

Eli knew most of the Native people had different legends of creation, but that most believed in a greater power they called by many names, but Creator was the most common. But God had given his Word and commanded those that have His Word to share it around the world with all people that have not heard, and it was that failure to do as commanded that allowed so many to go into eternity without ever hearing the true Word of God. He thought of so many that had a belief in a Creator, but he knew it took more than just believing He exists, for His Word speaks of the need for more in James 2:19 *Thou believest there is one God; thou doest well: the devils also believe, and tremble.* But how could he explain to this man that had held his belief all his life, that it would take more?

Eli looked at the old man, frowned, and asked, "You believe in the Creator, don't you?"

Long Walker let a slow grin split his face, "I do. I have always believed in the Creator." He chuckled, "And more...I knew a man, a white man, that told me of the Word of God. His name was Daniel Lee. He and his uncle, Jason Lee, came to our people when I was a young man. Daniel was my friend and he told me I must receive the gift of eternal life that Jesus bought for us on the cross." He paused, chuckled, "He told me if I did not accept, that I would not go to Heaven. I asked him, 'Is Heaven for both white men and Natives?' He said, 'Yes! It is for all who accept Jesus.'" The old man smiled at the memory, looked at Eli, "We prayed together, and I accepted Jesus as my Savior and received that gift of eternal life. Now I know that when I leave this place," motioning around him with wide swinging arms, "I will be in Heaven."

Eli smiled, nodding, "I am glad to know that, Long Walker. I, too, know that I will be in Heaven one day. I just hope it's not too soon!"

Both men laughed together, and Eli poured the rest of the coffee into their cups to savor before turning in for the night. Dusk had dropped its curtain of darkness and the stars were lighting their lanterns as if engraving their invitation to Heaven.

———

IT WAS LATE AFTERNOON, the second day after meeting Long Walker, that Eli pushed Rusty to the crest of the tallest butte that overlooked the town of Astoria. The setting sun was painting the water with gold and stretching long shadows from the tall masts of the sailing ships anchored in the harbor and the many buildings of the town below. Eli stepped down, dropped to his haunches, and with binoculars in hand, scanned the burgeoning town. To the west of the town, another butte held several skeletal snags of once majestic spruce that had somehow escaped the scalping of hillsides by the lumber hunters. The long shadows of the snags pointed to the many clapboard buildings, some two and three stories tall. Most were single-storied structures, and the main business section appeared to be near the docks where several tall ships were moored.

Knowing the reputation of Astoria as a wide-open and wicked town, Eli decided to wait until morning before he entered the lap of civilization. This was the mouth of the Columbia River, although another river some were calling Youngs River flowed in from the south to merge with the Columbia before the waterway met the Pacific. The smell of saltwater was in the air, yet Eli could also smell the stench of the city's sewers and more. He looked at Lobo, who had bellied down beside him, rubbed his scruff and glanced up to Rusty, "I think we'll be more comfortable here in the trees, don't you?"

CHAPTER 7

INQUIRY

E li was involved in the State Rights Democrat newspaper, reading about the president's veto of the Freedmen's Bureau Bill and the bitter haggling among Radicals and the Conservatives in congress and the views of the different newspapers that believed they spoke for the people. He shook his head at the stated arguments of the necessity of providing money, supplies, property and more to the displaced and recently freed slaves, mostly in the south. He was all for the rights of every man, but believed it was also the responsibility of every man to earn his own way in life. He had repeatedly been taught by his father that "with every right, comes responsibility. If you fail in that responsibility, you surrender that right." He chuckled as he flipped the page and began reading the many advertisements of businesses in the northwest of Oregon. He glanced up to see a man watching him, looked back at his paper and reached for his coffee, recently refilled by the waitress that had served him and answered many of his questions. Movement nearby caught his eye, and he lowered the paper to see the man from the other table coming his direction, looking directly at him.

"Excuse me, but I couldn't help but overhear that you are looking for someone?"

Eli nodded, motioned for the man to be seated as he answered, "That's right," without elaborating further. The man was dressed as a business man, dark suit, starched collar with a tie, a waistcoat with watch chain showing, and spats on his shoes. His hair was pasted down, parted in the middle and dark, while a thin moustache decorated his upper lip. He extended his hand to shake, "I'm Wilbur Courtright, and you?" he asked as he shook hands.

"I'm Elijah McCain," answered Eli, motioning to the waitress for more coffee. She brought another cup for Eli's guest, poured both cups full and retreated.

"Perhaps I might be of some assistance," began Courtright, reaching for his coffee. "I'm familiar with Astoria and the various businesses. I am one of the local barristers and make it a point to be informed. Who were you looking for?" he asked as he replaced his coffee cup in the saucer.

Eli took a deep breath, looking at the man, wondering just what he was up to, for he seldom found anyone so eager to be helpful without wanting something in return. He reached into his pocket to retrieve the tintype and began explaining to Courtright about his runaway sons. "I've been on their trail for some time now and have always been a little behind," surmised Eli.

Courtright looked at the pictures, glanced to Eli, "Are the boys in trouble?"

"No, it's not like that. I made a promise to their mother and just want to give them the news of her death."

"I understand. Have you made any headway in Astoria so far?"

"No, but I've just begun. I checked into the hotel here," looking around at the interior of the dining room of the Occident Hotel, where he had taken a room after stabling the horses in the livery. Eli looked back to Courtright, "The last word I had about my boys was that they were thinking about maybe getting on with a sailing vessel. They had inquired of the captain of the steamboat they were working on, and he talked to them about the different ships."

"I see. Well, my advice would be to begin with the different ship's agents along the waterfront hereabouts. Perhaps they might tell you of any additions to the ship's crews, although not all agents are privy to that information, they tend to stay focused on the cargo and passengers."

"Yes, I'm familiar with them and I do intend to talk to those that I can find." Eli was looking directly at Courtright, but movement behind the man caught his attention. He frowned when he saw the waitress motioning to Eli. She was frowning and pointing at Courtright and shaking her head.

Eli's expression caught the attention of Courtright, and he turned around to see what Eli was looking at, but the waitress had turned her back and was pouring coffee for another customer. Courtright looked back at Eli, frowning, but Eli reached for his coffee cup as if he had seen nothing. "You say you're familiar, do you have experience with sailing ships?" asked Courtright, trying to be nonchalant in his inquiry.

"My family are shipbuilders and I've had my time on board a few."

"Oh, and where was that, if I may ask."

"On the eastern seaboard, McCain Shipbuilders, on the Essex River. We build Schooners."

"Interesting," replied Courtright, nodding as he took another sip of coffee. He replaced the cup, reached into the pocket of his vest and withdrew a business card, placed it on the table between them and said, "I must be going. If I may be of help, in any way, please stop by, and I'll do all I can." He stood, extended his hand, "I wish you luck in your search." He shook hands with Eli and walked away.

As soon as Courtright had exited the dining room, the waitress, Amy, returned to Eli's table and said, "I was trying to warn you!" she declared, speaking softly as she gathered some of the dishes and cups from his table.

"Warn me? Whatever for?" asked Eli.

"Well, after you told me about your boys, and I saw that man come to your table, well…" she began, looking about and appearing busy, "I just had to tell you. We don't know for sure, but that man represents himself as an attorney, but mostly he's known as a crimp for some boarding houses."

"A crimp?" asked Eli, frowning and glancing around.

"Yes, a crimp. That's a man that drums up business for boarding houses by being the first at the docks when a new ship comes in or when a steamer comes down. He gets the crew to jump ship on promises of better jobs on another ship, good rates and *other promises* on shore and gets them rooms at the boarding houses. Then the men get drunk and shanghaied!"

Eli frowned, "Other promises?" he asked.

"You know, drinks and painted women, you know the kind," mumbled Amy, her embarrassment showing red at her neck.

"Do you know of men being shanghaied?'

"All the time. When they jump ship, the captains keep their wages, and the new ship's captain gives their advance wages to pay the bills at the boarding houses. That way, the men are in debt from the first day on board the ship."

"You seem to know a lot about the shady business, why is that?" asked Eli, always the skeptic.

"My brother was shanghaied, and that's what my father found out about how it's done. That was two, almost three, years ago, and we weren't sure until we got a picture postcard from New York from him. He said he had been shanghaied when he was at the Silver Quarter Tavern, here in town."

She stepped back, looking about, and moved closer to speak softly, "And that man was the last man my brother talked to before he was gone." She gathered up the dishes and marched off to the kitchen, leaving Eli with more questions than he had answers. He finished his coffee, left a five-dollar gold coin for Amy's tip, and settled his bill as he went out. He stood on the board-walk that fronted the hotel, looked to the many docks and several ships, and turned to start along the walk that fronted most of the business buildings that faced the waterfront, for that was where the agents for the ships could be found.

Most of the buildings that were near the waterfront were built on pilings and the streets were corduroy because of the logs and planking that rode the crest of the tide land. He learned that it was not unusual for some businesses, in particular the taverns, to have trap doors that opened to the water underneath and there was enough water for small boats to maneuver about under the buildings. This was the way many of the men were shanghaied—drunken, they would be knocked over the head, dropped through the trap door to a waiting boat, and not wake up until at sea.

Most of the agents served several ships, although usually those of the same ownership, and their records were minimal. The few that kept records of crewmembers, usually only had information on the captain, the navigator, and the other officers or first mates. None had been able to give any information about his sons.

It had been a tiring afternoon, but he was resolved to continue his inquiry after he had himself a bit of supper. Then he would make the rounds of the taverns, knowing that the local watering holes usually had more information than anyone in town, and if there was any news, that would be where he would find it.

He stepped into the High Tide Café and took a table near the window. A matronly woman with a frilly apron came to his table with a big enamel pot of coffee, poured him a cup, looked at him and with one hand on her hip, "Yeah?"

"What's the special?" asked Eli, grinning at the woman and waiting for his answer.

"Same," she grunted, scowling at him.

"Well, since I've never been in here before, same as what?"

"Same as always. We got fish, fish, an' more fish. Also got some clams. Oh, yeah, we also got crab."

"What kind of fish?" asked Eli, politely.

"Salmon an' halibut."

"Are the crab fresh?"

"Of course. Best Dungeness crab anywhere."

"Then I'll have the crab."

"Hmmph," grunted the woman as she turned her back on Eli and strode to the kitchen.

The meal was plenteous and tasty, and Eli leaned back in his chair, his hands resting on his belly as he smiled broadly at the woman. She saw him looking at her and turned away but soon appeared again with the coffee pot. Eli placed the tintype of his boys on the table, turned to face her as she approached, and pushed the coffee cup closer to the edge of the table as she neared. She saw the tintype, looked up at Eli, "What's that about?" she grumbled.

"Those are my sons. I've been searching for them and the last word I had was they were headed this way, might try to get on the crew of a sailing ship. I was wondering if you might have seen them, it would've been sometime in the last month or two."

She scowled at him, looked at the tintype, set the coffee pot down and sat down in the chair opposite Eli as she picked up the tintype. "They don't favor you."

"No, they favor their mother. She passed away but not before eliciting a promise from me to find them and try to get them to return home."

"Seen 'em."

Eli leaned forward, elbows on the table, "You've seen them?"

"That's what I said. Don't remember much, but they come in here a couple times, couldn't help but notice they bein' twins an' such, an' they was talkin' 'bout gettin' outfitted for sailin'. Don't know much else. Good lookin' boys, reminded me of muh own."

"You have a son?" asked Eli.

"Sons—two of 'em. Lost 'em both. Ship went down at sea." She shook her head, reached for the edge of her apron to wipe a tear, "Hope ya' fin' 'em!" she declared, standing and turning away.

Eli called after her, "Do you remember any ships at

dock about that same time, maybe one they might have signed on with?"

She turned back, frowned, "Only one I 'member was the Flying Cloud, a clipper ship. I think it was here 'bout that time."

"Thank you, I greatly appreciate that."

"Good luck," she stated as she turned on her heel and disappeared into the kitchen.

———

WHEN ELI STEPPED from the café, he looked at the waterfront at the different vessels moored and anchored. He spotted two schooners, one barque, a brigantine and a clipper. All but the clipper and one schooner were at the jetty or docks with longshoremen busy loading. Most of the cargo was freshly milled lumber bound for the southern coastal towns, but a variety of cargo decorated the shoreline, awaiting the vessels for transport. Although the news of the boys being seen by the woman was encouraging, he wanted more and committed himself to making the rounds of the waterfront taverns, hoping for additional information, or perhaps confirmation that the boys were taken aboard the clipper, Flying Cloud, either willingly or shanghaied.

The sun was lowering in the western sky and beginning to share its colorful glow that would soon turn the waters into molten gold, a sight that Eli always enjoyed and appreciated. He turned to the west, facing the sun, to begin his tour of the tidal taverns. He had already passed three, and knew there would be more, but also knew there were several away from the waterfront that could lure unsuspecting men. And so it was, he came up empty with those on the water, but when he turned to town, the biggest tavern, the Seafeldt Corner Tavern, yielded a bit when the bartender, in an idle moment, commiserated with Eli, and admitted to seeing his boys.

"Yeah, they were in here. All excited about possibly gettin' signed on a ship. But what they didn't know was too many o' them ships don't take inexperienced men. They want sailors that been to sea an' know what they're doin'." He looked at Eli, who slowly nodded his under-standing, then with a look about to see if anyone was near enough to hear, lowered his voice and said, "Now, you din't hear it from me, but there's a couple them clipper ships that are allus lookin' fer newbies they can train like they like 'em. If'n I was you, I'd be fer lookin' after the Flyin' Cloud. Ever since they set that record, they can't keep their crew from jumpin' ship. Seems ol' Cap'n Creesy an' his woman, who's his navigator, tend to be a little hard on their crew. So, I heerd they don't mind takin' on a shanghaied newbie or two, know what I mean?"

"I do," answered Eli, leaning on the bar. He looked at the bartender, saw him move back with wide eyes. Eli spun on his heel and stepped to the side just as a belaying pin slammed down on the edge of the bar with a loud crack that caused both the bartender and Eli to jump back. Eli knew this was the usual tactic of a shanghai crew, but he was ready. He brought his elbow back to smash into the face of the man that wielded the belaying pin, knocking him back from the bar just as a second man tried to grab Eli from behind. Eli snatched his Colt from the holster and swung wide to bring it across the side of the head of the man behind him, drop-ping him across the bar as he screamed and grabbed the side of his head that was spurting blood.

Eli spun around, looking for others, saw one man

hightailing it out the door, and turned back to the first man with the belaying pin. His assailant growled, lifting the pin shoulder high, "I'm gonna bust yore head wide open fer that!" he roared and charged toward Eli, but Eli feinted with the pistol, brought his knee up into the man's crotch and hammered down with his pistol on the man's neck as he stumbled. The man fell on his face in the sawdust-covered floor, spilling the brass spittoon over his face and arm.

The second man stepped back from the bar, holding the side of his head and ear as blood trickled through his fingers, growled at Eli, "You're gonna die for this!" and staggered out of the bar. Eli looked at the man on the floor, up to the bartender, "Did you have anything to do with this?"

"No, no! I just saw 'em comin'. Din't have time to warn you!"

"Ummhmm, yeah."

"But what that'n said, he means it. If word gets out you done these two in, they'll be sendin' more. If'n I was you, I'd be fer makin' muhself mighty scarce!"

Eli nodded, slipped his Colt back in the holster, "Was that true—what you said about the Flying Cloud?"

"Yessir, it was, an' to be honest, I saw these two," nodding to the man on the floor, "in here 'bout the same time I saw yore boys. An' the Cloud left the next day."

CHAPTER 8

CHANGE

"Jubal! Jubal! Wake up!" demanded Joshua, shaking his brother awake as he looked around in the dark, smelly compartment.

"Wha…wha…What're you doin'?" asked Jubal, pushing back on Joshua's hands and arms, fighting his way free of his brother as he tried to clear his head. He rubbed his eyes, shook his head, and looked around the dank hold. He stretched his arms to the side, trying to steady himself as he closed his eyes and shook his head. "Where are we?"

"I dunno, I just came to myself. It's too dark to see anything," started Joshua, falling back against a big cargo box with a coil of rope lying on top. He fought to sit up, still looking about, but the floor pitched and rolled under them. Boxes, gear, and rope tumbled about, knocking them down and landing atop them.

"We're on a ship!" declared Jubal, pushing a coil of rope off his legs. "And this ain't no steamship! We're at sea!" he barked, scowling at his brother as if it were his fault.

"At sea? How? We didn't sign on anywhere, did we?" asked Joshua, glaring at his brother.

"No! Wait. We were sent to that tavern, the one on the corner, by that Ship's agent. You remember?" asked Jubal, trying to right himself, his arms outstretched to keep the cargo at bay.

"Yeah, yeah, I remember. He told us to look for the First Mate of the Flying Cloud. But he wasn't there, was he?" answered Joshua.

"No, no, but the bartender said we could wait if we had a drink, and we asked for beer, but he gave us both a mug, but he called it grog, remember? He said it was rum, weak rum, remember?" recalled Jubal, shaking his head and rubbing his forehead. "I have a bad headache, you?"

Joshua frowned, "Yeah, I do! But I also have a knot behind my ear that hurts."

"I do too! That's it! We've been shanghaied!" declared Jubal, trying to get to his feet, but falling back. He frowned as he heard the slosh of water, looked to the beams overhead, and as his eyes were adjusting, he squinted to see the laps of the hull. He heard a moan from beyond a crate and crawled up to look into the darkness. Three other men, still unconscious, but appearing to come awake, lay in a pile between some cargo boxes. Jubal motioned to his brother to come up and look. "There's three others. Bet they been shanghaied too!"

A sudden shaft of light from above and a booming voice startled them, "Ahoy below! All hands on deck! Look lively now!" The shadowy face disappeared, but the light showed a ladder. Jubal said, "We better go," he glanced over to see the other three stirring and called to them, "Hey you three, we better go up top 'fore they come after us!"

Mumbles and grumbles, some sounding like questions, came from the pile, but Jubal and Joshua were already starting up the ladder, fighting their way against the pitch and roll of the ship. Joshua moaned, "I think I'm gonna be sick," he mumbled as he followed his brother.

Jubal answered, "No time for that now. The man said, 'Look lively,' and you know what can happen to a hand that doesn't obey!" He climbed through the hole and was blinded by the bright sun, although it was still on the rise and the clouds dimmed the glare somewhat. He stepped onto a deck that was awash with sea water, looked above to see unfurled sails and a pitching and rolling sea with whitecaps chasing one another. Most of the crew had gathered before the poop deck, whereupon stood what Jubal presumed was the captain and other officers. He gave Joshua a hand and the brothers staggered toward the gathered crew, shaking their heads and squinting their eyes, trying to stay erect as the deck rolled beneath them.

The captain motioned the men close, stood before and above them on the poop deck, and began his usual *before the voyage* talk. "Most of you men are aware, but there are some new ones aboard, so here goes...I'm the captain, Josiah Perkins Creesy, Jr., this," motioning to the two men beside him, "is the chief mate, Mr. Finch. He has the port watch. That'n is the second mate, who has the starboard watch, Mr. Koch. You new men, you three," motioning to the late arrivals from the bilge, "will be on the starboard watch, and you two," nodding to Jubal and Joshua, "will be on the port watch with Mr. Finch. Our voyage will take us to several ports on the west side of California, then south to Panama. We'll turn about and come back north with new cargo and passengers. Now, we have sixteen passengers aboard, and you men will have nothing to do with the passengers and you would do well to avoid them at all times, unless ordered otherwise, understand?"

The crowd of men nodded and answered with a hearty "Aye, Aye, Captain!"

He continued, "You are expected to obey orders and do your duty without question. We only have men aboard this ship," he paused, nodded to the navigator, "except, of course, for our navigator…and you will be expected to perform your duties like men! If you fail, the consequences will be severe! Those of you that are new, learn fast, do as you're told, and you will fare well!" He stepped forward, hooked his thumbs in his coat and inflated his chest, "To your watch!" he barked, and the men scrambled about the deck.

Jubal and Joshua watched the First Mate, saw him coming down the steps from the poop deck and walked toward him. He began barking orders to the others, looked at the twins, looking from one to the other and growled, "You two related?"

"Yessir," began Jubal, but the Mate interrupted, "Don't 'sir' me! It's Mr. Finch!"

"Yes, Mr. Finch, we are twin brothers. I'm Jubal, he's Joshua," replied Jubal, nodding to his brother and looking at the mate.

The Mate looked from one to the other, then turned and barked at his men, "Simon! Kent!" motioning the men to come to his side. As they stood before him, "Simon, you take that'n, he's Jubal. Kent, that'n, he's Joshua." He looked at the brothers, "You're their shadows, whatever they have you do, you do it!"

The brothers nodded, looked at the two men, and as they motioned, the brothers followed. Simon growled over his shoulder, "I'm the third mate, but don't go callin' me mister, it's Simon! First thing ever' mornin' we wash down the decks, we scrub 'em and scrape 'em with broom an' canvas, then we wet 'em down, an' holystone 'em. You two will have prayerbooks, an' I'll be showin' you how to use 'em, you'll be followin' the holystones an' get where they can't!"

———

THE FORTY-MAN CREW was all over the ship with brooms, canvas, and several manned the holystones, the smooth-bottomed, large sandstone with ropes on both ends that were drawn across the decks, sliding the length of the decks, to sand the wet-down planks. Jubal and Joshua were instructed with their prayerbooks, smaller holystones, to get into the smaller crevices and other narrow spots too small for the larger stones. Once most of the deck was done, the pumps were put to use and the sand washed off the decks, followed by the mops and the squeegees. Once the decks were dry, eight bells were sounded, and the men turned to for their breakfast.

Jubal and Joshua were rolling their shoulders, rubbing their arms, and looking at their hands as they walked together to the galley for their breakfast. They looked at each other and heard the mate telling the others, "You've got thirty minutes for your breakfast, then turn-to and we'll finish the job! We've got five boats to clean and polish and all the brass to polish 'fore inspection!"

After breakfast, both watches returned to their duties about the ship with five small boats and more to put in order. The work was divided among the crew with most assigned work about the ship with some to polish the brass, others to clean the stanchions, some the steps of the forecastle and hatchways with the holystones, and more. Jubal and Joshua were again put to work with the prayerbooks, or small holystones, and their hands were red and sore, and beginning to appear raw. But two bells sounded the end of the first hour of the forenoon watch and the chief mate called out, "All hands, prepare to get underway!"

The crew scattered to their assigned tasks, most of the men appeared anxious to do their job and all knew their duty as most turned to at the task of raising the anchor. As soon as the anchor was hove short, the mate shouted, "Loose the sails!" and the crew scrambled to the rigging and up the shrouds and out on the yards, ready to let go the sails.

"You! With me, stick to me like you were tied!" demanded Simon as he motioned to Jubal and started to the Mainmast.

"You! Just like them!" ordered Kent as he started at a run to the Mizzenmast.

The men scrambled up the rigging and shrouds and out on the yards of their assigned sails. Jubal and Simon were on the Main Topsail and Joshua and Kent were higher on the Mizzen mast at the Mizzen topgallant sail. Simon signaled for Jubal to hold while he moved out on the yard to cast off the yard-arm gaskets and bunt gaskets. Once they were loosed, he motioned for Jubal to take to the yard on the starboard side, "Do as I do, when I do it!" he shouted. Simon grabbed the bunt jigger, moved out on the yard and motioned for Jubal to do the same. Each man grabbed an arm full of sheet and a hand on the halyard. Simon looked below and listened as the mate shouted, "All ready fo'rd?" and the crew answered with "Aye, Aye!" The mate continued with, "All ready main?" and continued with the mizzen, then "Let 'er go!"

In short order, the tall masts that had stood like skeletons, blossomed with loose canvas and crew began to slip below, save one man on each top to sheet the sails home. The rest of the canvas was loosed, both watches busy at their tasks, and as soon as the yards were trimmed, the anchor was weighed, and the ship was underway. When the Flying Cloud was under full sail, the mate barked, "Go below the watch!"

Simon motioned to Jubal to go, and he was followed by Joshua. They looked at one another, started for the hatch that would take them below and without a word, they slipped down the ladder, dropped into the steerage and felt their way in the dim light from above to find their duffels and sort their gear. They were exhausted and had only stood one four-hour watch, but the other three newbies came close, and one man spoke, "I'm Whitcomb. This is Riley and James," pointing at the other two. Riley and James appeared to be about the same age as the brothers, but Whitcomb looked to be in his upper thirties. Whitcomb continued, "I've sailed before, but this is the first time for these two. You?" he asked.

"It's the first time on a sailing vessel for us, but we've served on a steamship or two," answered Jubal.

"Well, good. Then we can help each other." He looked around, "Ain't much here, but what usually happens, after you prove yourself, you'll earn a bunk in the crew's quarters, but that could take a while. Best make ourselves comfortable here, as much as we can anyway," he resolved. "First off, we need to try to stabilize the junk down here so we can make a place to sleep. Wanna give me a hand?" he asked, looking at Jubal.

As the two set about moving the crates, the others gathered the loose gear and castoffs, placing them further away and they soon had a reasonable place cleared. Whitcomb had spotted a corner that had several crew trunks and said, "Those are from other crew that are not on the ship. They usually gather up their left-behinds and put 'em in a trunk or two so new men, like us, can pick through them and get a little better outfitted. Wanna have a look?" he asked, speaking to the others.

It took no encouragement for the others to join in the rummaging and within a short while, each man had doubled his gear of seaman's clothing and felt much better prepared for their voyage. They sat about for a short while, sharing their stories and getting acquainted. All had been shanghaied from the same corner tavern, but the other three had no plans to sign on to crew a ship like the twins. They were surprised to hear the brothers were glad to be aboard, just not happy about how they got here. Whitcomb spoke up, "Well, men, we best try to get some rest. We've got just a couple hours 'fore we'll be called back up top!"

CHAPTER 9

SOUTH

T he sun was tucking itself below the western horizon, leaving behind the glimmer of gold and red that gleamed and bounced off the ripples of the river, as Eli walked down the boardwalk bound for his hotel. He had looked forward to a hot bath, soft bed, and a warm room for the night, but he was troubled by the news of his sons shanghaiing. By experience, he knew being a part of a ship's crew aboard a sailing vessel, would not be an easy voyage. Ship's captains often saw themselves as the god of their vessels and often ruled mercilessly. With some captains, the slightest offense would result in thirty or more lashes, and with some, hanging was the ultimate punishment for breaking the law aboard the ship, and that law was whatever the captain deemed. As he walked, he remembered his own experience that was tempered by the fact he was the son of the shipbuilder and owner, a privilege that any shanghaied crew would not enjoy. But he also knew any pursuit of a clipper would be a fool's errand.

He shook his head as he thought, considering all his

options and the possibilities of finding his sons. Based on their recent behavior and habit of quitting on their commitments, he thought the boys would probably jump ship at the earliest opportunity, for what they might have thought to be a great adventure would probably become a miserable experience they would want to end as soon as possible. With a glance to the eastern sky, he saw the early rising full moon and decided to go to the livery, check on the horses and Lobo, maybe take them out for a stretch of the legs. He always thought better in the saddle.

Lounging in a rocking chair by the door of the livery was the old-timer that owned the stable, he said his name was Calvin Gregg. He was a wiry-looking man, clean-shaven, grey hair and piercing dark eyes. He had buckskin britches, a loose hanging homespun shirt, and high-topped moccasins. He nodded to Eli as he approached, "You wantin' yore horses already?"

Eli grinned, "Dunno. Thought I'd check on 'em, maybe take 'em out for a stretch of the legs. I always think better in the saddle."

"Yup, know what'chu mean. That's the way it is with me too, only nowadays I don't do as much thinkin' as when I was a young'un," he chuckled. He frowned at Eli, "What's got'chu so discombobulated?"

Eli chuckled at the expression, knowing it was an apt description of his thinking, "Well, I found out about my boys," he started, pausing to look at the old-timer.

"Good, good! Where they be?" he asked, looking around as if expecting to see them behind Eli.

"Shanghaied!" grumbled Eli.

The liveryman, Gregg, shook his head, "Happens," he paused as he looked up at Eli, "So, now whatcha gonna do?"

"That's just it—I don't know. The ship, the Flying Cloud, is headed south with ports of Eureka and San Francisco, before going on to Panama. And even then, there's no telling how long the boys will stay aboard. They tend to not stick with anything very long and might be jumping ship at the first opportunity. I thought about tryin' to catch up with 'em, but that's a fool's errand."

"If'n they was to jump ship, where'bouts you think they'd do it?" asked the old-timer.

"Prob'ly San Francisco. You know, young men, big city and such, sounds like a fun time."

"Ummhmm. Mebbe you oughta go down the old trapper's trail, what some call the Siskiyou trail cuz it crosses the Siskiyou mountains on a pass south o' here. That'll take you there, but you won't get there 'fore the ship, mebbe soon after, take ya' at least a month, mebbe longer."

"Siskiyou?" asked Eli.

"Yup. It's the trail the Hudson Bay boys used, 'course like all the others, it was a Injun trail first. Lotsa gold hunters used it both ways, some goin' down there, like I done, others comin' this way a mite later when gold strikes were made up north hyar."

"You traveled it—goin' after gold?" asked Eli skeptically.

"Wal, I were a bit younger then..." he shrugged, grinning. I joined up with ol' Seth Kinman an' done some pannin' on the Trinity. Din't do so well, so we went to the coast, started huntin' for Fort Humboldt. That's where we met a young shavetail name o' Ulysses S. Grant!" he chuckled. "Got tired o' fightin' them grizzlies and got me passage on a steamship what come north to Astoria, been here ever since! Now ol' Kinman, he started makin' chairs outta elk antlers and bearskins, give some of 'em to the different presidents!"

"Does that trail over the Siskiyou Pass go all the way to San Francisco?" asked Eli.

"It do! That's why the Hudson Bay folks used it. They'd send a brigade o' trappers south n' they'd trap the mountains an' such, keep goin' to San Francisco, sell the furs and come back the same way or catch a ship to come back to Fort Vancouver. Fella by the name o' Young made him a bundle bringin' horses an' mules north o'er that trail to sell to the settlement hyar in Oregon. Then he'd go back, get a herd o' cattle, do the same thing. Made out real well, he did. 'Course that was 'fore the gold rush, an' 'fore they fixed the road for the stage-coaches. Now there's even some places what got the tele-graph connected." He shook his head at the thought of civilization creeping north.

"Where would I get on the trail?" asked Eli.

"Oh, ain't nuthin' to that. Just ask anyone in Portland or Oregon City. They all know it. Most of 'em use it time an' again. It goes south along the Willamette River an' such." He scowled and looked at Eli, "I'm gonna be lockin' up hyar directly, so if'n you want yore horses, now's the time to make up yore mind."

Eli looked at the man, "I thought you might have a history in the mountains, buckskins and such, but it's not often I see a man with a livery in town that spent his life in the mountains."

"Hehehehe," he cackled, "Wal, young'un, I never wanted much. Just kinda went with the flow of things, ya know? Only wanted to do three things - see the moun-tains, kill me a grizzly, get some gold, an' ride on one o' them steamships. Done 'em all, hehehehe."

"Uh, that's *four* things," said Eli.

"Yup. Ain't ever'body what gets to do more'n they set out to do! Now I just sits hyar, let fellas hand o'er the money, an' if'n they need sumpin' done, got ol' Mose back thar that's the best blacksmith this town ever seen, and he can fix just 'bout anythin'. Together, we can do it all. I got the brains; he's got the brawn. Make us a purty good pair!" He looked at Eli, "Oh, I meant to tell ya' 'fore we got to jawin', there was a couple fellers hyar checkin' to see if'n you had horses hyar. Din't like the look of 'em, so I tol' 'em I ain't never seen nobody like they was talkin' 'bout. I think they was some o' them shanghai bunch."

Eli chuckled, "Yeah, I had a little set-to with a couple of 'em back at the tavern. They weren't too happy and, like most, made a lot of threats as they helped each other out of the place." He shook his head, looked at the old man, grinning.

Gregg looked at Eli, up at the rising moon, "I allus like travelin' in the light o' the moon. There's a side-wheeler docked down yonder," nodding toward the waterfront, "that'll prob'ly be goin' upriver, mebbe e'en tonight. That'll gitchu to Portland sooner."

Eli frowned, "What's the name of it?"

"It's the Wilson G. Hunt. Been here 'fore, goes upriver to the Cascades an' back again."

Eli grinned, "I met the captain, John Wolf, isn't it?"

Gregg nodded, "That's him. Good man." He looked at Eli, "If'n you were to do that, you could outfit in Portland or Oregon City 'fore you take the trail south."

"Sound like a good idea. I'll get my horses."

———

Captain Wolf was standing at the bow, watching the longshoremen and his crew finish loading the cargo that was bound for points upriver. He saw the rider coming toward the boat and frowned, but when Eli neared, John recognized him and called out, "Eli! Never thought I'd see you hereabouts. Weren't you looking for your sons?"

"Still am," answered Eli, leaning on the pommel of his saddle. "Looks like you're getting ready to push off."

"Soon, real soon. I want to make time with the full moon, cut the travel time by a good spell 'fore we hafta take on more wood."

"Got room for a passenger and a couple horses?"

"I do! We have several stalls we've used for horses and cattle and such, most are full of cargo, but we have some empty ones that should suit you. Also have a couple cabins open. Goin' far?"

"Just to Portland. Then I'll be headin' south."

"Might get a boat goin' up the Willamette from there," suggested the captain.

"Well, we'll see when I get there. It would cut down on the travel time a mite, I reckon."

"How far south you goin'?" asked the captain, watching Eli dismount and start leading his animals to the gangplank.

"Dunno, maybe San Francisco. Depends on what I find. My boys were shanghaied, and if I know them, they'll be jumping ship the first opportunity."

"Happens all the time. I've lost some crew to the shanghai bunch. Every time somebody whispers the word *gold*, the crew gets all wide-eyed and hopeful and think they can get rich with little or no effort. Sometimes, all it takes is the promise of a new adventure."

Eli nodded, "Oh to be young again and concerned about nothing but adventure!"

"Yeah. I'm 'bout ready to retire from 'adventure' in favor of a rockin' chair and a good woman."

Eli chuckled, "All you gotta do is get a pocketful of gold!"

CHAPTER 10

UPRIVER

"Cast off port!" called the captain, followed closely by, "Cast off starboard!" and the big ropes thudded on deck, followed by the crewmen. The big 'steeple type' steam engine began to chug and huff as the piston rod rose and fell in the guides to move the pair of pittmans to turn the wheels. The water splashed, the boat hull groaned and the 185-foot-long *Wilson G. Hunt* began to pull away from the docks. The captain's telegraph rang and was answered, and within moments the clarion bell rang, the engine paused, and the paddlewheels groaned and churned water again, pushing the boat into the current of the wide Columbia River.

Eli had stripped the gear from the horses, put Rusty and Grey into two stalls, tossed them some hay and stowed his gear nearby. He walked about, noting the unique features of the *Hunt*. The pilot's house was forward on the Hurricane deck, the single smokestack towered high behind the pilot's house, and behind the stack was the wedge housing for the piston rods, unusual for the time since the *Hunt* had the old style 'steeple type' engine, said to be safer than the usual engine used by most riverboats. The main deck held the corrals and stalls for livestock, cabins at the aft, and the second deck, often referred to as the boiler deck, or in the case of the *Hunt*, it was the hurricane deck—had more cabins and the galley for the small dining room. Although there were fewer than usual passengers, the captain said they had 32 passengers, the captain had offered Eli a cabin, but he chose to make his bunk near the horses, keeping Lobo near and out of trouble.

After his self-guided tour of the riverboat, Eli returned to the stalls and stacks of cargo to make himself a bed. With his bedroll over his shoulder, he pushed and shoved at some of the bales and boxes, arranged himself a bit of a bunk, and began stretching out the bedroll when he heard, "Welcome, señor!"

Eli looked up to see a man leaning against the bulkhead, a sombrero pushed back on his head, and rolling a cigarette, grinning as he lifted his eyes to Eli.

"Thanks! You bunkin' nearby?" asked Eli, finishing his bed-making and standing erect to look at his visitor.

"Si, si," he answered, nodding behind him, "there. I made mine much like yours." He glanced at the horses and nodded approvingly at the big claybank stallion, "I, too, prefer the company of my horse to that of strangers." He looked behind him to another stall that held a buckskin Criollo stallion. The horse tossed his head, showing his long and well-groomed mane, his nostrils flared, and his eyes were bright. Eli noticed much the same response from Rusty, as was the way of stallions when they meet another.

Eli extended his hand, "I'm Elijah McCain."

His visitor grinned, lit his cigarette, accepted Eli's

hand and shook it, "And I am Candalario Bernardino Navarro. It is good to make your acquaintance, señor McCain."

"Eli, please. Just Eli."

"As you wish, Eli. And most call me Candy," he grinned, took a puff on his cigarette and asked, "Have you had dinner?"

"No, but I didn't think this boat had a dining room."

"Oh, but it does. Please, join me," he stated, motioning for Eli to lead the way as he pointed to the stairs.

At the table, the conversation turned to the getting acquainted manner. It started when Candy asked Eli, "You have the stature of a military man, were you in the war?"

"I was, but I had served for several years before that in the west, stationed at Fort Laramie during the time of fighting Indians and making peace treaties. Then the war came, and I was shipped east. You?"

"No, no. As with the rest of the country, there were those in the north that were against slavery and those in the south that were secessionists. But my people, on the Rancho Monte del Diablo, were cattle people. Señor Pacheco believed it was our responsibility to support the Union with beef, but the only way to get cattle to the war was by ship and that did not prove to be dependable. There were some that joined the California regiments, but my family has served the Rancho and the Pacheco family for three generations, and I could not leave them." He paused, took a long draught of coffee, looked up at Eli, "Now, I am scouting a route to bring a herd of cattle north to the settlers and gold hunters."

"Oh? A route for a cattle drive, any one in particular?" asked Eli.

"The Oregon-California trail, what some call the Siskiyou Trail, is the only one I know about. I know there have been herds driven on the trail, but we have not, and it is best to know the trail. To take a herd of more than a thousand is a great risk, and we must be certain."

"I am taking that same trail south as well," began Eli, as he started to explain his quest to find his sons and their subsequent shanghai. "The trail was recommended by a man that traveled its length, but that was some years ago. My goal is to get to a couple of the harbors to find out about the ship and perhaps my sons. I know I cannot make the same time the clipper might, but …". he shrugged, reaching for his coffee as he glanced at Candy.

"Then perhaps we might accompany one another on this mutual quest," suggested Candy.

———

THEY HAD BEEN on the river for two days when the dim light of dusk was fading, and the *Hunt* nosed into shore just upriver from the little settlement of Eminence. Two crewmembers splashed ashore, the tether lines hanging heavy on their shoulders as they worked their way to the big trees that would be the tie-off for the night. The first mate, Ryder, watched as the stage was lowered over the bow. Once secured, he turned back to Eli, "She's ready!" he declared. The two men had remembered their first encounter and had intentionally avoided one another. Eli stood with Rusty and the grey, followed by Candy and his mount, *Atardecer*, Sundowner, close behind. The two men led their horses to the grassy flats just beyond the sandy shore and picketed them to graze on the tall grass that waved in the evening breeze. The men found the trunk of a downed cottonwood and took a seat to watch and wait for the horses to get their fill.

Eli looked at Candy, "So, tell me about this rancho where you work."

Candy chuckled, "It is not just where I work, it is my home. My family, padre, madre, dos hermanas, uno hermano, all live and work there. It is nuestra casa." He paused, chuckled, "Did you not have a home, family?"

"Yes, I had a home, but my only family was my mother and father. There were no siblings. Our home was on the east coast, my family, my father and his brother, were shipbuilders, and I grew up on the water." He dropped his eyes as he had a brief moment of reminiscence, looked up at Candy, "And the rancho?"

"Ah yes, it is a beautiful place. With Walnut Creek on the west, the foothills of Mount Diablo on the south, the Carquinez Strait on the northeast. It has many acres of beautiful rolling grassland, fertile valleys and the mountains at its back. It was a grant of almost 18,000 acres to the elder Salvio Pacheco over thirty years ago. But he had lived on the land before that, and my grandfather and my father served the patron."

"Sounds like a magnificent place and fine home. Were all the men in your family vaqueros?"

Candy frowned, stood erect, his heels clicked together, and he expanded his chest, threw back his shoulders, "I am not a vaquero! I am a Charro! A Charro is a greater horseman than any mere vaquero! This," he motioned with a sweep of his hand from his shoulder to his boots, "is the clothing of a true Charro." He lifted his shoulders and stood with his chin up and eyes looking below to the boat. His heavily brocaded bolero was tailored to his frame, the long sleeves with fine fringe, the brocade covering the chest, the short jacket hanging open to show his loose white linen shirt. The butts of two Colt Navy .38 caliber revolvers showed when the jacket hung open. The tailored trousers were tight fighting and of the same black material as the bolero, a brocade stripe going down the outside of each leg, but the armitas, or leather chaps, covered the trousers, yet flared open at his boot tops. He was a handsome and pompous figure as he stood proudly.

Eli let a slow grin split his face as he nodded at the man before him, "All that and you do not have a *prometido?*"

Candy was surprised at Eli's use of the Spanish to speak of a fiancé. He looked at his new friend, "I am still looking for a *mujer hermosa*. I cannot settle for just anyone!"

Eli chuckled, "No, I suppose not. Someone as prideful as you must have a beautiful woman that will add to his standing as a great Charro." He grinned as Candy fought to keep a straight face but failed.

Candy relaxed, laughed, and sat back on the grey trunk of the long-dead cottonwood. He looked to Eli, "You are not too old to find another, why do you not?"

"I guess I'm a little like you, just waiting for the right one." Eli looked at the horses who stood, looking back at the boat and around. They were not alarmed, just curious. Before the men brought them from the boat, the horses were saddled and had the bridles hanging on the saddle horns. Eli walked to Rusty, slipped the bridle on over the loose-fitting halter, tightened the girth, and looked at Candy as he also put the bosal on his mount, and was ready to ride. He swung aboard, looked at Eli, "See if your crowbait can keep up with my magnificent Criollo stallion!" He dug spurs in the ribs of the buckskin and launched toward the trees where a narrow trail split the thick trees.

Eli grabbed the saddle horn, "Go, Rusty!" he challenged and before his feet left the ground, Rusty sprang ahead. Eli lifted his feet together, swung them forward and let them fall together, driving them into the ground, using the momentum of the horse to swing up onto the saddle and drop into the seat, leaning forward on the neck, his face in the mane, as Rusty gave chase to the buckskin. The trail cut to the west, twisting through the trees and rose up the face of a hill where a wide, open, clear grassy flat beckoned. As they drove through the trees, limbs slapped and sought to unseat the riders, but the experienced horsemen lay low, twisting and turning away from the branches and when they broke into the open in the wide clearing, Rusty was stretching out and pulling alongside Sundowner when Candy laughed and reined up.

Both men sat laughing, leaning forward to stroke the necks of their stallions, and the horses were prancing, tossing their heads, and giving each other the once-over. But the grey joined them, pushing between the stallions, nipping Rusty on the shoulder as if to keep him in check. Lobo had kept pace with Rusty and was laying on his belly, his tongue lolling, as he watched the men and horses before him. Candy frowned as he looked at Lobo, "Is that your dog?"

Eli chuckled, "He's a wolf, and it's more like I belong to him than the other way around. He seems to have adopted us some time back," motioning to himself and the horses, "He keeps himself scarce, not really a friendly mutt, but he's a good friend."

Candy looked at Eli, shook his head, and said, "I've

never known a man that has a wolf for a friend—and two fine horses."

"That's a good mount you have there, he looks like an Andalusian, but I've never seen a buckskin Andalusian."

"He is a Criollo. They are from the Pampas in Argentina and Brazil. They are an ancient breed, but fine horses. Strong, fast, and great stamina. They are very good with cattle also." He paused to look at Rusty, "And yours?"

"He's a cross between a Morgan and a Tennessee Walker. He's the best horse I've had and, like yours, great stamina, speed, and great with cattle, although I've not spent much time using him with cattle. Now that one," motioning to the grey, "is a mustang, mountain-bred and raised. Got him when I was at Fort Laramie. He was a yearling when I took him east with me, thought I'd use him in the war, but..." he shrugged, "the army had other ideas."

The men rode in silence as they pushed back through the woods and the winding trail to return to the shore. They would spend the night on shore with the horses, giving them ample time to graze and enjoy the open spaces before getting penned up in the stalls on board for the next few days.

Chapter 11

Oregon City

Eli and Candy leaned on the railing of the hurricane deck of the *Hunt* as they passed through the town of Portland. With structures on both the west and east banks, new construction showed everywhere, making it evident the town was growing. The captain had turned the helm over to the pilot and joined the two at the rail. He observed, "Every time I come through here, there's more businesses, more people, and more riverboats!"

Eli asked, "Why more boats?"

"Don't you know? They're makin' 'em upriver here at both Canemah and Oregon City."

They had left the Columbia and taken the lesser Willamette River. Eli frowned, "That's the last thing I expected. Didn't this one come around the Horn?"

"It did. It was built by the Collyer yard in New York in '49. She was still new when the word came of the California Gold Rush, and she was sent round the Horn to San Francisco. Took most of a year, but she made it and Captain Burns had her 'fore I did, but she has since paid her dues." He leaned forward, nodding upriver, "The ships they're building upriver are for above and below the falls, most aren't as big as this'n, but I hear they're building some good ships."

"So, you're just going to Oregon City?" asked Eli, giving a sidelong glance to the captain.

"There are lumber mills and grist mills at Oregon City, and we'll be topping off our load with both. Those are valuable commodities up the Snake River, what with the gold camps and all," explained the captain. "Our sister ship, the Oneonta, will take the cargo east." He looked at the two men, "I expect you'll be disembarking at our stop?"

Eli nodded, "We will. Need to re-supply and then we'll be going south."

"Together?"

Eli chuckled, looked at Candy and Candy grinned, "Si, captain. We discovered we were going the same way and thought it would be good to travel together."

Captain Wolf nodded, "That's good. I try to keep informed as to what's happening on shore and apart from the Modoc, who are generally peaceful but lately are not too happy about being relocated to the reservation, and the Northern Paiute, who are thought to be a part of the Snake War that's going on, I've also heard there's a lot of bandido activity in the southern part of the state, northern California. And, of course, there are lots of settlers that are none too friendly and get a little hostile with strangers crossing their land."

Candy looked back to Eli, who chuckled, "Captain, you're just a bundle of good wishes, aren't you?"

The captain laughed, turned to lean his back against the rail, "Well, sometimes my world consists of these two decks and the water under the hull, so I like to keep abreast of what I might be missing out on."

"Tell you what we'll do captain," began Candy, "for every Native or bandido we come up against, we'll take a souvenir off their dead bodies and send it to you, just so you won't think you missed out."

"You do that, Candy. Just send 'em care of the *Hunt* either Astoria or Oregon City, and I'll be sure to get it."

The three men laughed together as they watched the boat plow its way through the waters, passing all the signs of progress and the hundreds of people involved in the growth. Eli was quiet as he watched, thinking this kind of civilization was reminiscent of a disease that was very contagious and continually spreading. And like many diseases, left a variety of scars in its wake.

———

SINCE ASTORIA, the *Hunt* had brought them over a hundred miles on the Columbia and the Willamette Rivers. After a long five days, now on the late morning of the sixth day, they were arriving at the docks of Oregon City. Most of the city stretched out on the east bank and appeared to be on a terraced hillside, with almost all the buildings on the riverbank level. Eli saw the big water wheels of mills near the falls, other industrial buildings nearby, but where they were docking, there were business buildings interspersed with residences.

The men had agreed to resupply and leave the town before nightfall, hoping to be free of the settlement before dark. They offloaded the horses and gear and started to the main street to find a mercantile or emporium to get the necessities. Eli asked, "Have you traveled this trail very often?"

"I have not, but I have studied and learned about it from those that have," explained Candy. "Mi padre knew a man, Ewing Young, who drove a herd over the trail when I was but un niño, a young boy, but I'm sure it has changed much since that time. They say there are stagecoaches that travel that trail now, so it cannot be too difficult."

At the Falls Mercantile, which had a faded sign on the side of the building that said *HBC Mercantile*, reminiscent of the days when most trading shops were owned by the Hudson Bay Company, they purchased the long list of supplies and talked with the clerk about the Oregon-California trail, but he was of little help, having seldom traveled away from Oregon City since he arrived by boat from San Francisco. Eli spotted an old-timer that appeared to be fingering some harness but was obviously listening to the men talking of the trail. The old man grinned, chuckled, and stepped near, "And jus' what is it you young'uns are wantin' to know 'bout the ol' trappers trail?"

Both men turned to look at the newcomer, and Eli answered, "We're thinkin' about going south on that trail and would appreciate anything you could tell us about it."

"Hehehe, if I cain't, ain't nobody can!" he answered, lifting his baggy britches over his paunch. "'Course my mem'ry works better when it's oiled up, if'n ya' know what I mean?" he cackled.

Eli looked at the clerk, who nodded, "He used to trap those hills and more, so he prob'ly knows as much as anybody," clarified the clerk, finishing the tally on the supplies.

Eli turned to the old man, flipped him a coin, "Alright old-timer," and nodded to the louvered dividers that separated the emporium from the adjoining tavern, "How 'bout you 'oil up your memory', and meet us outside where we'll be packing our supplies?"

The old man grinned a toothless smile and answered, "I do it, yessir!" and pushed through the swinging doors with a wave over his shoulder.

Candy looked at Eli, "You think he'll come out?"

"Depends on how much he can buy with a quarter," grinned Eli.

But the old man surprised them, stepping onto the boardwalk about the same time they did with their arms full of supplies. He cackled as he thrust two smaller coins into his pocket, licked his lips from the last of the foam on the beer in the mug he held before him, sat down on the bench in front of the window, and watched as the two packed their new supplies in the panniers and parfleche on the packsaddle aboard the grey.

When the men were tightening the ropes and straps, the old man began, "I first came north on that trail right after that cattleman from Californy, name o' Young, drove his herd o' cattle up to Portland. Yessir, that trail smelled like cow manure fer the next two years! Hehehe" he cackled, tilted his mug to gain the last drop of the beer, sat it down and continued. "We was trappin' the Umpqua an' Willamette fer Hudson's Bay Comp'ny. We came all the way from Fort Umpqua to Fort Vancouver." He went on to tell about the trail, where it followed the rivers, and over the mountains and more. After answering most of the questions from the two travelers, the old-timer, known as Bones, said, "Wal, young'uns, you have yerselves a grand time, just watch out fer the grizzlies and the hostiles! Hehehe," and disappeared into the tavern.

———

THE LOWERING sun was in their face as they came to the north bank of the Tualatin River. The river merged with the Willamette that was sided by the trail as they left Oregon City, but the Tualatin was running low, and the trail crossed a gravelly bottom about a half mile west of the confluence. The men reined up, but Eli stood in his stirrups, shaded his eyes from the setting sun, scowled and turned to Candy, "That looks like a camp, 'pears to be three or four wagons there at the edge of the trees. Maybe there's a place further on, or..." he shrugged as he looked at Candy.

"You thinking of camping with them?" asked Candy, frowning. "I thought you wanted to get away from civilization."

"Yeah, but don't you smell that cooking? Somebody's got themselves a woman that knows how to cook!"

Candy laughed, "Lead the way, amigo," as he motioned with a wave of his hand and grinned.

CHAPTER 12

COMPANY

"Hello, the camp!" called Eli as they came in sight of the wagons. He and Candy reined up to await an invitation and watched as two men, both with rifles across their chests, stepped toward them.

"Ja, come in if you are friendly!" came the reply.

Eli glanced to Candy and to the men as they nudged their mounts forward, keeping their hands before them, one on the pommel and the other holding the reins. "Saw your fire. We were getting ready to camp ourselves, thought we might share the clearing with you folks, if you don't mind."

"That is fine, ja. There is lots of room, and grass for the horses."

Before moving, Eli added, "I'm Elijah McCain, and this," motioning to Candy, "is Candalario Navarro. We're headin' south on the same trail and decided to travel together. You folks headin' south also?"

"Ja, ja. We are bound for San Francisco." The speaker paused, and added, "I am Anton Lund, and this," nodding to his companion, "is Leif Hansen. We have four families traveling south."

"Pleased to meet you both. And which one of you has the woman that's cooking something that smells powerful good?"

The men grinned, looking to one another, "All the women are good cooks. What you smell is the many different dishes. We often take the meals together." He glanced at his partner, who gave a slight nod, "You are invited too."

Eli looked at Candy, who was grinning and nodding, "That sounds wonderful. We'll make our camp and join you. Is there anything we can bring to add to the feast?"

"No, it is all provided. It will be ready soon."

Eli and Candy chose a spot just inside the trees, but enough of a clearing for graze for the horses and space for their bedrolls. It was close to the water for the horses to be picketed with grass and water but separated from the wagons by a narrow strip of hemlock, fir, and berry bushes. They wasted little time setting up their camp, stashing their gear and picketing the horses. And with a stern admonition to Lobo to stay with the horses, they started back to the wagons. "Whatever they're cooking, it sure smells good," declared Eli, glancing to Candy. They had taken a moment to freshen up, washing off and dusting off their clothes, although they had been on the trail for but a short distance. Eli noticed when Candy saw two girls, young women, who had looked wide-eyed at the visitors. He added, "Now, don't go getting too involved with those young ladies. Remember, we're only going to be here tonight. We'll be leaving early in the morning."

Candy chuckled, "Si, si. But it would be a shame for

me to deny the young ladies the opportunity to experience the love of an *amante charro.*"

Eli did not understand the words, but he could easily discern his intent by his manner and expression as well as the glint in his eye. He grinned at the Latin lover and shook his head, understanding the ways and wiles of the young. He guessed Candy to be in his mid-twenties, perhaps younger, and had already expressed his intent to find a woman to make his wife and build a life together.

A grinning Anton welcomed the two men to the gathering, motioning them to a large table that had been set up with boxes and planks, covered with linen and with benches and chairs arranged about. As they approached, Anton motioned to the others to gather about and began introducing the group. He spoke to the group, "This is Elijah McCain," but was interrupted by Eli, "Eli, please, just Eli." Anton nodded and continued, "Ja, Eli, and this is Candalario Navarro—" and was interrupted by Candy, "Candy, please."

Anton grinned, "Candy. Now, this is my wife, Freja, and this is Leif's wife, Olivia." The ladies nodded, smiling, and Anton continued, "This is Erik Pedersen and his wife, Alma." As he introduced each one, the men stepped forward to shake hands with both men, and Anton continued. "And this is Marcus and Ida Moller, and their children, Hannah, Soren and Tobias." The children were young, the girl about nine and the boys appeared to be about twelve and ten or eleven. Eli looked back to Anton, who continued with introductions of the children and went through the names of nine more children, but he also noticed the special attention shown by Candy to two girls who stood beside one another, Emilie Lund and Asta Hansen, both about sixteen or seventeen.

Eli grinned when Anton fell silent, and asked, "Please don't expect us to remember all these names."

Anton and several others laughed, "No, no. Of course not. But perhaps if you stay around a while, you might get to know everyone." Anton chuckled when he saw the look of confusion on the face of Eli, but Candy paid little attention as he was smiling at the young ladies. Anton motioned for the men to be seated as the other men were. Most of the youngsters were scattered on blankets and boxes and anxiously awaiting the food. The women began filling plates and were stopped when Marcus Moller stood, "Let us ask the Lord's blessing on our time together and the bounty He has blessed us with." He looked around at everyone until he had their attention, then dropped his head and began to pray, "Our Heavenly Father, we are grateful to you for your guidance, protection and provision." He continued with a rambling prayer that offered his thanks repeatedly but finally brought it to a close with, "And this we pray in Jesus' name, Amen!" His 'amen' was echoed by the others and conversation broke out and the ladies began setting filled plates before everyone. The aromas of the meal were pleasing and when Eli began eating, he smiled, looked at Freja and asked, "This is wonderful. It's new to me, but very tasty, what do you call it?"

Freja smiled, "*Hakkebøf* is what it is called in our homeland. Ground beef steak with spices, onions, boiled potatoes and pickled beets."

"It is delicious."

Anton chuckled, "Wait until you have her breakfast!" and smiled at his wife, who dropped her eyes, both proud and slightly embarrassed at the praise from her husband.

As the conversation continued, Eli learned the group

were all Danish and second-generation immigrants. Their families were all early settlers in Wisconsin and made their homes on farms and more. The plates had been emptied and taken by the women, coffee was poured, the women excused themselves to tend to the clean-up and the youngsters scattered to make themselves scarce with their many games. Eli asked, "So, you're looking for farmland?"

"*Ingen*, no. We are not farmers," replied Anton. He looked about, motioned to Erik Pedersen, "Erik and I are builders, Anton is a cabinet maker, and Marcus is a stone mason and pastor." He paused, chuckling, "We came here on the Oregon trail but not to farm. We are builders of communities and that is our desire." He glanced to the others, turned back to Eli, "We did some building in Portland and Oregon City, but we were not at home there. We also want to breed horses, our big horses," pointing to the grazing animals, all big draught animals, "We agreed we would try the cities along the coast of California or..." and shrugged. He looked at Eli, "And you? And your friend?"

Eli grinned, "We just met while onboard the *Hunt*, the sidewheeler we rode from Astoria to Oregon City. But we have become friends and we're both headed south, exploring the old Trapper's trail, or what some are calling the Siskiyou Trail." He went on to briefly explain about his search for his sons and Candy's exploration of the trail for a cattle drive.

"So, we *are* all going the same way," began Anton, grinning and glancing to the others. "Before you came to dinner, we had been discussing the need for someone that either knew the trail or could scout the trail for us. Although we came out on the Oregon Trail, we were a part of the bigger wagon train that had the scouts and more. We would like you and Candy to scout for us, you know, mark the trail, hunt some game, warn of danger, all those things. It would give our women more security, comfort if you will."

Eli glanced at Candy, but the younger man had excused himself and was walking toward the young women who had been looking his way. Eli chuckled, "It might be beneficial to both of us, but I'm not sure my belt could stand good cooking like this all the time."

"If you would talk to Candy, we will talk among ourselves and perhaps we could come to a mutually beneficial arrangement," suggested Anton, nodding to the other men.

"I'll do that," and he glanced at the darkening skies, noted the sliver of moon in the western sky and one bright star that seemed to stand alone in a black expanse, "Now, if you'll excuse me, I must check on our horses and make ready for bed."

"Breakfast will be shortly after first light," called Freja, smiling and waving as Eli moved away from the table and the light of the lanterns and the glow of the cookfires. Eli turned, smiled, and acknowledged the invite with a wave.

CHAPTER 13

CROSSING

Eli was not disappointed, but a little surprised, with the breakfast. Freja served a *rundstykker* or rye breakfast roll with a soft cheese and a thin slice of cured sausage. A soft-boiled egg sat beside the roll and as Freja poured the men some coffee, she motioned for Eli to partake. Candy preferred to tend to the horses and get their gear packed and ready, "I am seldom hungry when I wake, but later..." he shrugged, grinning as he watched Eli leave the camp, bound for the wagons and his 'surprise' breakfast. Lobo was at his heel as he entered the camp and the surprised family stared at the wolf until Eli introduced him, "Lobo, these are friends." He motioned for him to lay down beside him and with tentative steps and a vigilant eye, Freja served Eli. Now Eli was the one grinning as he bit into the breakfast roll with the tasty toppings, "It's very good, Freja, thank you," he declared.

Anton had joined him and as Eli ate, he asked, "What did you decide?"

Eli grinned, "Well, after Candy got acquainted with

your daughter and her friend, he didn't take much convincing. So, I reckon you have yourselves a couple scouts."

"Excellent!" declared Anton, glancing to his smiling wife. "Everyone will be glad to hear the news."

"But there's a couple things you need to know," began Eli, reaching for his coffee. "I've been around wagon trains and other campaigns with many people and it's important to know who's going to make the hard decisions. As scouts, many of those decisions as to when and where we travel should be up to us, but anything directly involving the people, we will defer to you. Is that acceptable?"

"Certainly. And with your time as a military commander and your experience in the wilderness, we are very willing to accept your judgement on such matters. We trust you," answered Anton, glancing to Leif, who had joined them.

Eli stood, picked up the last of his breakfast roll, nodded to Freja, looked at Anton and Leif, and said, "And there will be times when either Candy or I will be gone, but not at the same time. We have other matters to tend to." Anton nodded his agreement again, and Eli responded, "Then let's get ready to roll!"

Candy was leading the three horses, already saddled and ready, from their campsite when Eli and Lobo left the others. Candy stopped, watched Eli approach and asked, "Was the breakfast worth it?"

"Of course. It was very good, different, but good," answered Eli, accepting the reins of Rusty and the lead of the grey. He swung aboard and looked at Candy, "Remember what that old-timer, Bones, said about this trail? Didn't he say where the river bent south and then west, it was shorter to take the lesser trail southwest, come out at Boone's Landing and cross the Willamette on the ferry?"

"He did. He also said since the Willamette bears west before it turns south, rather than follow the river, we could bear southwest across the flats where there's so many farms and such, the trail's supposed to go straight southwest, and come out at Salem. But if I remember what he said, it'll be more'n one day to get to Salem."

Eli nodded, "You're right. But it is supposed to be easy travelin'. Since you're so interested in the girls, I might let you ride closer to the wagons while I take to the trees, sorta make myself scarce."

Candy grinned, "Oh, I'm sure I can handle things while you hide out!" he chuckled as Eli gave him a withering look.

With Mount Hood and the long stretch of the Cascade Mountain Range off their left shoulder, they started through the rolling hills with those that sided the Tualatin River, their first obstacle. The road they took angled across the face of the timbered hills, rounded a knob and cut over the saddle to break into the open for a short stretch, before splitting some thick timber and rounding another knob on the east side to drop into the wide open valley of farmland before them. The road was well-traveled but seemed to wander among farmland and scarred hillsides that showed stumps, both recent and weathered, where settlers had harvested the logs to build their homes and barns.

Eli was surprised to see a split log roadway across the boggy areas that would otherwise be challenging for a wagon to cross. It appeared to have been made a few years past and had seen considerable traffic, but was a welcome sight, nevertheless. By mid-morning they had crossed the split log roadway at Newland Creek and at

Boeckman Creek, bringing them within sight of the Boones Ferry and the little settlement of Boones Landing. The road stayed atop the high-rising bank before rounding a switchback and dropping to the ferry landing. A small cabin was tucked into the trees and belched a man who appeared native and greeted the wagons.

"Aho! Welcome to the Boones Ferry. Are you crossing today?" he asked, looking at the first wagon and leaning to the side to see the others close behind. Eli and Candy rode up to the man and Eli asked, "How much?"

The man pointed to a crudely lettered sign but gave Eli the prices, "Wagon and one team, two dollars, extra team, fifty cents. Each adult, twenty-five cents, child ten cents. Each man and horse, fifty cents. How many you got?"

Eli glanced back at the wagons, "Four wagons and teams, four extra teams, two men and horses, extra horse, eight adults, twelve children. By my estimation, that's fourteen dollars and twenty cents." He looked at the man who was trying to count on his fingers, looked up at Eli, "Sounds right. I can take one wagon and team, an extra team, and some people on each load."

Anton was driving the first wagon and heard the exchange and was digging into a lockbox for the money. With money in hand, he stepped down and paid the man. Eli nodded, "You start off, Candy will go with you on the first trip, I'll stay behind and follow up."

Anton nodded and started to unhitch the lead team, but the ferryman said, "That's alright, no need to unhitch. We'll put 'er in the middle, others on the side. Those are big horses, heavy too, but there's room."

Anton nodded and stood beside the team to lead them onto the boat. He looked at Freja, "Keep a good grip on the reins, but I'll lead 'em from here."

She smiled and nodded, sat with feet braced on the footboard, reins in hand, and appeared to be every bit the pioneer woman. Eli looked at the youngsters, "Emilie, you tend to the others and get aboard after the wagon is on, understand?"

"Yessir," she answered and gathered her little sister and brother close, watching the loading of the wagon.

Eli quickly calculated and decided each ferry trip would accommodate the wagon and two teams, two adults and three children, with one carrying the pack-horse and he would take the last one with Rusty. He stepped down and directed the others as they took their place in line, each standing to watch the crossing of the ferry.

With big logs as the frame, planks for the deck and saplings for the railing, the ferry had been in service since 1846 and had been reworked and improved several times over the years. Long oars with locks on the rein-forced railing were handled by oarsmen from the Tualatin Kalapuyas Indian tribe, whose native land had been taken by the Donation Land Claim Act of 1850. A big cable stretched across the waterway, running through big metal rings screwed deep into the log frame, and was kept taut by the weight of the ferry against the current. Most of the native people had been moved to the Grand Ronde reservation, but several remained behind to eke out a living working for the white man.

The first and second crossings were easily done and the third wagon, that of the Moller family, was soon loaded with the entire family, including the daughter, Hannah, and the two brothers, Soren and Tobias. Eli led the grey packhorse aboard, tethered him to the rail, looked at Soren, the oldest of the boys at twelve, and asked, "Would you keep an eye on my packhorse? He might get a little nervous, so all you need to do is talk to him and maybe stroke his neck a little, alright?"

Soren smiled broadly, pleased to be given the responsibility, and answered, "Yessir. Will do, sir!" and stepped closer to the horse. His little brother asked, "Can I help too?"

Eli grinned, "Of course, just don't get too close. I'm sure your brother can handle him fine." Eli walked off the ferry and turned to watch as they pushed off into the current.

Ida Moller stayed on the wagon, as did the other wives, and Marcus stayed at the head of the teams, calming the horses. The boys were on the upstream side of the ferry and, as most boys do, fussed at one another, each wanting to stay close to the packhorse. When Tobias fussed as he pushed at Soren, his brother pushed back and hollered, "Ma! Get Tobias away from me!"

Ida leaned over to look at the boys who were out of sight from the driver's box. She moved closer to the side and scolded Tobias, "Toby, leave your brother alone. Come on now, you get on the other side here," she demanded.

Toby grumbled, dropped to his hands and knees to crawl under the wagon and stood on the other side. As he started to the driver's box, the current of the river caused the ferry to shift slightly, and Toby stumbled, grabbed at the rail, and with a scream from his mother, who was leaning to the side to watch, he splashed into the water.

The river was deep, the current strong, and the boy splashed about frantically. His mother screamed, "Marcus, Marcus! Toby fell over!" she was shouting, standing and holding on to the bows of the wagon and pointing, looking from her husband to the river. Marcus was holding the horses who were skittish, prancing about because of the screaming and shouting, and he struggled to hold the horses still, looking from the front of the ferry to the water, to the splashing boy, and to his wife. He knew if he let the horses go, they could easily kick about and maybe even crash against the railing and drag wagon and all into the river. He was torn between steadying the horses, saving his wife and older son, and diving into the water after Toby.

The oarsmen near where he went over shouted and pointed, trying to get the attention of those on shore, but they could not leave their oars for that would hinder the forward progress of the heavily loaded ferry, and without that forward motion, the current could push all the weight against the stationary ferry and might break the cable, which had happened before.

On shore, Eli saw the boy go overboard and quickly swung aboard Rusty and dug heels into his ribs to rush down the shore, keeping an eye on the thrashing boy. When he had raced past the boy, he slid the big claybank to a stop, slipped his pistols into the saddle bag and leaped from the saddle into the water. He spotted the last point where the boy was seen and paddled furiously to that location, but the boy could not be seen. More screams and shouts could be heard from the banks, but Eli was focused on the water. He twisted and turned, kicking with his feet and moving his hands about to stay above the water, but he could see nothing. He bent at the middle and dove into the current, trying to keep his eyes open in the murky waters, looking for any sign of the boy, but he could only see a short distance, and there was nothing but bits of debris floating with the current.

He kicked and came up for air, looked around frantically, and dove deep again. His search was unsuccessful, and he kicked about, feeling and trying to see, but there was nothing. Coming up again, he splashed about, twisting and looking around, kicking against the current. He looked on shore, lifted his hands in a sign of despair, and heard shouts and cries, but none could give any direction. He tried again, but again his search was futile. He shook his head, looking about, and reluctantly swam back to shore. He staggered onto the shore, stood with hands on knees and hanging his head, trying to get his breath. He went to his horse, grabbed the saddle horn, stepped into the stirrup and mounted. He twisted about to look at the wide river that stretched all of two hundred yards wide with a strong but deceptive current. Although the water looked placid, the occasional piece of floating debris revealed the swiftness of the current.

He sat, leaning on the pommel, and looking at the water, knowing the boy was gone. He breathed heavily, shoulders lifting, and nudged Rusty to move along the shore and continue downstream, watching the current for any sign of the boy. He had gone about a half-mile further when he spotted a floating snag and a flash of color that was out of place caught Eli's gaze. He frowned, watching the slow-moving and rolling snag of a long-dead tree. *Maybe*…thought Eli. He couldn't tell for sure, but he had to check. He nudged Rusty at a faster pace than the current, loosing his riata and taking it in hand. He nudged Rusty into the shallows, and as the snag neared, he swung the rawhide loop overhead and tossed it to the log, catching the upright limb. He dallied the riata around the horn and pulled on the reins, "Back boy, back," he directed Rusty, who began backstepping, pulling the riata taut as the current tugged at the snag. As the weight of the log swung closer to shore, Eli nudged the big stallion to the shallows and the slope of the bank, dragging the snag closer. Once the snag was grounded, Eli stepped down and ran to the log to find a waterlogged boy, unmoving, but slowly breathing. He spat, coughed, stirred, and Eli snatched him up and with his face away from him, Eli squeezed the boy hard, expelling a surge of water, and the boy coughed, stirred, spat, and coughed again, sputtering and fighting.

Eli laughed, dropped to his knees on the sandy embankment, and lowered the boy, turning him around and looking at the bright-eyed but waterlogged boy, who was still coughing and struggling. "You go right ahead and spit and cough, boy!" he laughed and slowly stood. As Toby struggled to stand, Eli picked him up and sat him on his saddle, climbed up behind him, and swung Rusty around to start back to the ferry landing, relieved and happy, hugging the boy tight and holding him against his chest to get the shivering boy warm.

CHAPTER 14

FLATLANDS

This was the Willamette valley, the fertile lands that attracted so many settlers to give up their homes in the east for farmland in the west. This was the valley that brought thousands across the country on the Oregon Trail, to fight hostiles, weather, hardship, disease, and more, just on the hope of finding land that could one day be their home. All about them were the signs of settlers, cleared fields, planted and even harvested fields, stumps that scarred the land where once towering trees grew.

Some of the land they passed had workers busy at removing stumps and leveling land, preparing it for the next spring's planting. Homes of all sorts stood next to barns and other outbuildings, most made of logs, some of lumber, and in as many different styles and colors as the variety of people that occupied them. As Eli rode silently, looking about at the signs of settlement, he knew at one time, not so long ago, this had been the wild land of native peoples, many that had been obliterated by the diseases of white men like small pox, cholera, measles, and more, while others had been decimated by attempts to remove them by untold massacres with the remaining few forced to give up their tribal lands in favor of small spots on a reservation.

To Eli, although these were the signs of advancing civilization, he did not believe these were signs of a superior people, but rather of a cruel and selfish people. He shook his head in shame for his fellow man but knew there was little, if anything, he could do about it all. It was late afternoon on the second day after the river crossing when they bypassed Salem on the east side, continuing south. The timbered mountains to the east were crowding closer and those on the west of the Willamette shouldered nearer the river. In the distance, masked by the haze of late afternoon, he could see the distant mountains and he longed to be away from the flats and back in the mountains.

They crossed the Santiam river, rounded Knox Butte, bypassed Albany, and were approaching the Calapooia River that flowed in the shadows of Petersons Butte, when they were approached by several riders. Eli had gone well ahead of the wagons and Candy rode beside the lead wagon of the Lund family, talking with Emilie, who sat beside her father on the wide seat, her feet resting on the footboard. Three men reined up in the middle of the wagon road, two leaning on their pommels, one sitting tall and holding his hand high to stop the wagons.

Candy spurred his horse forward, approaching the men. He pushed his sombrero off his head, letting it dangle on the chin string at his back. He smiled broadly as he greeted the three men, "Hola amigos! Why do you stop us? Is there a problem?" he asked, looking from one to the other.

The man in the center grinned and looked at Candy, "Yes, there is a problem. This is a toll road, and the crossing of the river is a toll crossing. For you and your wagons to go further, you must pay a toll."

"Oh, I did not know that. And just what is this toll?"

The man grinned, leaned to one side and the other, "You have four wagons?"

"Si," answered Candy, watching the three men.

"Then the toll is two hundred fifty dollars."

"Two hundred fifty dollars? Hmmm, that seems to be a lot of money."

"Oh, but you do not understand, that is $250 per wagon. That means the toll is $1000!"

The man grinned as his two compatriots laughed, looking to one another. Candy could see they were well armed, but none had their weapons drawn. As he looked from one to the other, the leader added, "I see you are looking at us, thinking about whether to pay or not. That would not be smart. You see, we have more men in the trees…" he turned to motion to the trees and two more men rode into the open and continued to move down the road on either side of the wagons, looking at the families and the wagons. They held rifles across the pommels of their saddles, pointed toward the wagons, grinning as they moved down the line.

Candy leaned forward on his pommel, his hands dropping close to the butts of his two revolvers that sat inconspicuously on his hips under his bolero jacket. He grinned as he looked at the speaker, "And if we do not have that much money?" he asked.

"Then we will take your stock, your women, and anything else we want," growled the leader threateningly, "And I will personally take that young woman right there!" pointing to Emilie, who sat beside her father and laughed with the others.

Behind them came a calm voice from Eli who had come from the woods at river's edge. He had seen sign of several riders, rode into the shallows, and turned back into the trees. When he heard the movement of several horses, he lay low on Rusty's neck, watching as three of five men, talking low between them, started to the road. He stayed hidden until the other two men rode from the trees to join the others. He was within earshot and sight of the three highwaymen when they made their demands, and he knew Candy had spotted him as well. As the men spoke, Eli slipped his Winchester from the scabbard and muffled the sound of cocking the hammer with his free hand, then pushed Rusty to walk slowly up behind the three.

"You won't take anything if you're dead!" declared Eli, his voice calm and natural, but loud enough to be clearly heard.

The three startled men turned in their saddles to see who was behind them, grabbing at their holstered pistols as they turned, but Eli's rifle barked and spat fire and lead, driving the bullet into the sternum of the leader's chest. The rifle bucked, but Eli jacked another round at the same instant Candy's pistol roared and knocked the man to the left of the leader from his saddle. Eli's second round smashed through the neck of the third man, driving him onto the mane of his horse that spooked, jumped and dropped his head between his feet and kicked his hind feet at the treetops, unseating the bloody rider, dropping him on his face as the horse took off to the trees.

Eli hollered, "The other two, you go that way, I'll take this one!" pointing to the right side. He jacked another round into the Winchester as he slapped legs to the big stallion. Candy had jerked his buckskin's head around, dug spurs into his ribs and rounded the lead team of the Lund wagon. The two horses, although separated by the wagons, were running neck and neck the short distance to where the other two men, alarmed at the shooting, had jerked their mounts around and were starting to the head of the wagons, but when they spotted riders charging toward them, they lifted their rifles to fire.

A shout came from the wagons, "NO! Don't shoot!" It was just enough to catch the attention of the two outlaws and gave enough of an edge to Eli and Candy, both of whom had charged the length of the wagons and now came sliding to a stop. As the outlaw in front of him started to turn to shoot, Candy's Colt lifted and bucked, but the bullet creased the side of the outlaw's head, and he grabbed at his head, lowering his rifle. His hand came back bloodied, and he lifted his hands to the Charro, started to lift his rifle, but Candy's pistol barked again and the man slid from the saddle, dropping his rifle on the far side as he grabbed his chest, looked at Candy with wide eyes, and landed in a patch of cactus at the edge of the road.

Eli, the experienced cavalryman, slid Rusty to a stop but kept his rifle lifted and both rifles roared, the outlaw's shot was hurried, Eli's was not. The outlaw took the slug just below his ribs on his left side, and blood blossomed. The shooter looked down, saw the blood, lifted his eyes to Eli, tried to talk, but he lost his grip on the rifle, letting it clatter to the ground. He fell forward on the neck of his horse, who spooked to the side, coming out from under the rider and dropping him to the ground.

Eli watched the man fall, breathed deeply, called out, "Candy? You alright?"

"Si amigo. This one is dead, you?"

"I'm alright. Get some help and drag these cretins into the trees, loose their horses if they're not wanted, then come to the front."

"Si amigo." He looked up at the nearest wagon, driven by Marcus Moller, "Will you help me, señor?" Marcus nodded and handed his wife the reins, stepped down as Candy looked at the last wagon, "Señor Pedersen, will you help also?"

Eli returned to the lead wagon where Anton Lund was comforting a sobbing Freja and asked him and Leif Hansen to help him with the dead. They pulled the wagons to the side of the road and jumped down to help Eli. The men worked in silence, digging shallow graves and covering them with rocks and branches. They were filling in the graves when the rattle of trace chains, the clatter of hooves, and the splashing of wheels in the water brought their attention to the road where a stage coach drawn by a six-up was pulling to a stop. Eli looked at the men, "You finish here, I'll talk to them." Eli walked to the stage, nodded to the driver who asked, "You folks having trouble?"

"Not now, we did just a bit ago, but it's over with."

"You buryin' somebody yonder?" asked the driver, looking to the trees where the men were finishing their task.

"That's right. We had a bunch of highwaymen that thought they were goin' to make this a toll road and demanded we pay a thousand dollars. When we said we didn't have it, they threatened to take the women, stock and anything else they wanted. I told them no, they started shooting and came out on the losin' end of it."

The driver shook his head, looking about, frowned when he saw the horses standing near the trees. He looked at Eli, "That horse belong to one of 'em?" He was looking at a flashy sorrel with flaxen mane and tail, four stockings, and a silver mounted Mexican saddle.

"Yeah, it was ridden by the man doin' the talkin'. He was the one that started the ball and the first to die."

"Well mister, I don't know who you are and don't really care, but that horse belonged to a bad man name o' Winifred Vaughan. Him and his cousin are some kinda back door relation to the outlaw, Hank Vaughan. His cousin, Harvey Smith, is the sheriff o'er to Albany, and he has an office in Brownsville too. Most folks think he's just as bad as the rest of the family. I don't know what he'll do, but he won't be happy to find out about his cousin yonder." He paused, looked at Eli, "If'n I was you folks, I'd be makin' tracks outta this country!"

Eli looked up at the driver, over to his messenger, "Thanks for the warning. There wasn't anything we could do, short of gettin' shot, and I just wasn't in the mood for lead poisonin' today."

"Can't say as I blame ya!" answered the driver. He looked at the others, glanced at the wagons, nodded to Eli, "We got a schedule to keep. Good luck!" He drew back his bullwhip and cracked it over the heads of the six-up that leaned into their collars and dug hooves into the road. The trace chains rattled, the coach rocked back on its thoroughbraces and they rose a small cloud of dust as they headed north on the road.

When all were ready, Eli motioned to the others to follow, and they crossed the Calapooia River. Once across, there was a fork in the road with a sign pointing west that read, *Brownsville 5 miles*, and another on the same post pointing south, *Eugene City 25 miles*. Candy caught up with Eli and looked at him, "Should we tell someone in the town about those men?"

"Did you hear what the Jehu of the stage said about those outlaws?"

"No, I was finishing the grave diggin'. What'd he say?"

"The leader of this bunch is the cousin of the sheriff in Albany and Brownsville who is as big of an outlaw as this'n. I doubt if they'll be missed very soon, but if we say anything, we'll do it in Eugene City."

CHAPTER 15

GABRIELLE

The *Flying Cloud* hove to and lay becalmed outside the mouth of Coos Bay. At the direction of the agent, the *Cloud* anchored offshore of the Cape Arago lighthouse. The agent was bound to go into Coos Bay and deal with the Simpson lumber mill and shipyard to make arrangements for future cargo of lumber and more. With the ship becalmed, the hatches had been removed and the air in the steerage was fresh and cool, unusual for the sailor's quarters. It was two bells of the last dogwatch, or seven o'clock in the evening, when the mate came down to the steerage, grinning like a Cheshire cat, "Ho boys! I have the steward and his fiddle ready for a good time! Who's with me?"

The announcement was met with a chorus of cheers as the men rolled from their berths and followed the mate to the 'tween decks to hang the light and begin the dancing. The steward was quick with his bow and brought more music from the four string fiddle than most had ever heard, but their feet began the dancing and jumping. The floor deck had been made smooth with the holystoning and the second mate set his boy to dancing with a sailor's shuffle and a fisherman's jig. Most of the men joined in, slapping bare feet on the boards, jumping as high as the decks would allow.

The music was jolly and loud, and Jubal and Joshua had joined in the fun. They had locked arms and were kicking up their heels when Jubal looked to the hatch to see two young women, passengers, watching and tapping their feet and clapping as they enjoyed the dancing and cajoling. Jubal made a swing around, told his brother to look, and both men waved at the girls, motioning for them to join the fun, but the girls laughed and shook their heads, preferring to watch from above.

Eight bells marked the end of the last dogwatch and brought an end to the dancing. With a glance to the hatch, Jubal saw the women had disappeared, undoubtedly gone to their cabin, for they were cautioned not to mix company with the sailors. He shook his head, grinned, and remembered other times he had seen, even caught the eye of, the two girls. He elbowed his brother, "You've seen them before, haven't you?"

Joshua chuckled, "Yes, and every time I try to say something, they're gone before I can think of what to say!"

"You always were tongue-tied when it came to women," Jubal chuckled, thinking and remembering the women, "They look like sisters, you think?"

"Well, they both have blonde hair, if that's what you mean?"

"No, it's more than that. They just look alike, not like us, you know, not twins, but maybe sisters."

"Uh, before you start hatching some kind of plan to meet them, you better remember what the captain told us. We, none of the crew, are to have anything to do with the passengers."

"That's easy for him to say. He has his wife with him!" replied Jubal as they returned to their berths. He was referring to Eleanor Creesy, the navigator for the *Flying Cloud* and the wife of the captain. They would be called at middle watch and that was less than four hours. Jubal flopped into his berth, turned to the hull and mumbled, "Maybe we'll see 'em later."

"I thought so!" declared Gabrielle Devereaux.

Her sister, Gisèle, frowned, "You thought what?"

"I thought they were twins. I had seen them before, but never together, and each time, there was a little difference, now I know why! They're two different men!" she laughed giddily, looking to her sister. "Don't you see? We've imagined having brothers for our mates, and to have twins? It couldn't be any better!" she giggled.

"They *were* funny, dancing together, if you could call what they were doing, dancing," laughed Gisèle. The girls were in their berths in their cabin. They were traveling with their mother and were bound for San Francisco to see their mother's sister for a short visit with family, then would return to Monterey to their home. Their father had made his fortune in the California Gold Rush with a strike near John Fremont's rich diggings but had lost his life when the riverboat *Colonel Wright* was overrun near Fort Walla Walla. The boat was hauling all the makings for a luxurious gambling hall and saloon, complete with a number of dance hall girls and entertainers, and when the word got out, local woman-hungry men stormed the boat and overran those that tried to defend the women, among them was John Robert Devereaux, the girl's father, who gave his life in defense of the women, women who eagerly accepted the many proposals of single farmers and miners and made a home away from the dance hall business. He was on his way to the most recent gold strike in Montana aboard the *Colonel Wright*, but he left his family financially comfortable.

———

SIX BELLS on the morning watch saw Jubal and Joshua as crew of the gig under the direction of the coxswain, Whitcomb, and the other two crew were Riley and James, all newcomers to the crew of the *Flying Cloud*. The gig was to be used by the agent to take him ashore to deal with the Simpson lumber mill and shipyard for future cargo. The light whale-boat was freshly painted and the brass polished. The stern seats allowed for up to six passengers while the crew were in the bow with the coxswain at the rudder with the bowman in charge of the boat-hook.

Jubal and Joshua sat facing the first row of seats, backs to the bow and hands on their oars and the tholepins in place, when the ladder came over the side to allow the passengers to board. First off was the agent who always gave the impression of self-importance and arrogance and was disliked by all the crew, but he was followed by three women, Gabrielle, Gisèle, and their mother, Geneviève Devereaux. The women were seated side by side in the front row of seats, leaving the back row just in front of the coxswain to the agent.

Captain Creesy, who was well known for putting the safety of the ship above all else, had refused the agent when he demanded the ship to be taken into Coos Bay, explaining the Bay was uncharted for a Clipper Ship and he would have to go in by gig, but the distance to the shipbuilder and sawmill was considerable, making the crew of the gig work especially hard to breach the rollers and waves at the mouth of the bay, but breach they did and were soon into the smoother waters of the bay.

"My, you men are so‑strong, to handle the boat the way you did. I'm impressed," spoke Gabrielle, giving a coy smile as she talked, looking directly and boldly at Jubal. Joshua had kept his eyes on Gisèle, as the girls sat on either side of their stern-faced mother.

"All in a day's work, miss," answered Jubal, giving a half smile under one raised eyebrow. "I'm Jubal, and this is my brother, Joshua," he added, nodding to his brother and glancing from Gabrielle to Gisèle, intentionally avoiding eye contact with the mother.

"Well, young man, I am their mother, and I have tried to keep my daughters in hand and have demanded they avoid any contact with the crew of the *Cloud*, as per the instructions of the captain. However," she continued, glancing from Jubal and Joshua and back, "since it is evident that our lives and our safety are in your hands, perhaps it would be best if we were not complete strangers. Jubal, Joshua, I assume you have surnames?"

"Yes, ma'am, Paine," answered Jubal, pulling on the oar in time with the others.

"Jubal, Joshua, these are my daughters, Gabrielle," touching the arm of the girl on her left that sat opposite Jubal, "and Gisèle Devereaux. I am their mother, Geneviève Devereaux."

"Very pleased to meet you, ma'am, ladies," answered Jubal, nodding to each in turn. He was copied by Joshua, who added, "Likewise, ma'am, ladies."

"And what does your father do? Is he also a sailor?" asked the woman, looking sternly at Jubal.

"No, ma'am. Our natural father died before we were

born, he was a career soldier. But he asked a West Point classmate and friend to take care of his wife, our mother, and they were married shortly after. His name is Elijah McCain, *Colonel* Elijah McCain. He too was a career soldier, but we were raised on our mother's ancestral home, a horse ranch in Kentucky where some of the best horses are bred and raised."

"Oh, I see. But you said your step-father *was* a career soldier, he's no longer a soldier?"

"No, ma'am, he retired from the army after the war was over."

"And did he return to the farm?"

Jubal glanced to his brother, and Joshua explained, "We don't know ma'am. You see, we were also in the army, joined shortly before the end of the war, and after we got out, we wanted to see the west and have been doing just that ever since. The last we heard from our mother was she was expecting him home soon, but we haven't heard anything since."

"And what prompted you to become sailors—more of that *wanting to see?*"

Jubal chuckled as he glanced to Joshua, waiting for him to explain, but Joshua deferred to Jubal who began, "Well, sort of, we were thinking about signing on with an ocean-going ship, our step-father had spoken of it before—his family were shipbuilders, and we had crewed aboard a steamship on the rivers—so we thought we'd give it a try. Then one day, we woke up aboard the *Flying Cloud,* and here we are!"

The coxswain had turned the gig toward the docks below the settlement of Empire City, where the agent believed the Simpson Shipbuilders and Sawmill had an office. It was the nearest settlement and the only one with any stores for the ladies. As the gig bumped the jetty, the bowman jumped out and tied the gig taut, then stepped to the side and gave a hand to each of the ladies. He cautioned them, "Now ladies, when the agent returns from his business, he'll be wantin' to get back to the ship, so don't dawdle. We can't waste any time now, y'hear?"

Mrs. Devereaux glared at the bowman, glanced at the twins and looked back at the bowman, "We will not be ordered about by you! Do you understand me?" she spoke sternly as she scowled at the man. She turned back to look at Jubal, and Jubal answered, "Don't you worry, ma'am, we'll be right here when you're ready!"

"Good, see to it, young man!" she ordered as she popped open her parasol and led the way for the feminine shopping mission.

Jubal glanced at the bowman, then to the coxswain, rolled his eyes and mumbled to Joshua, "Sure hope they're back 'fore the agent!"

CHAPTER 16

MOUNTAINS

He was a peddler of women's corsets and other unmentionables, and there was only one store, the Brownsville Emporium, that handled his wares. He opened his case and catalog on the counter, wiped the sweat off his brow, looked back to the fly-specked front window and nervously turned toward the owner. The peddler was a fidgety little man, but the owner, Horace Woodson, had dealt with him before, and although he was the typical obnoxious peddler, Horace noticed he was a little more nervous than normal. "So, Mr. Beauregard, what seems to be bothering you on this fine day?" he asked.

The peddler looked up at the owner, who stood with his gartered white shirt, string tie, and long canvas apron and a broad grin. "It's just, just..." Beauregard stammered, turned to look through the window that faced south directly across the street from the Sheriff's office and the *Trey of Spades* tavern. "Is the sheriff in today?" he whimpered.

Woodson frowned as he looked at the peddler, a short

but round man with a serge suit that appeared to have fit him about thirty pounds ago and the buttons on the vest were straining to keep from losing their hold on the threads that were about to pop. His bald pate was usually covered with a derby, but the round top sat on the counter beside his sample case. Woodson shook his head, "No, he went to Corvallis to deliver a two-bit horse thief. 'Tween you an' me, I think he's just wantin' to get the reward money, but he said he wanted to see the outlaw get his due and he wanted to see the man hang. He said he'd be back in a couple days. Why?"

"Oh, nuthin', I s'pose. Just somethin' I heard while I was on the stage." He paused, flipped some pages in the catalog and looked up at Woodson, "Is the sheriff related to a fella by the name of Vaughan?"

"Yeah, I think they're cousins, why?"

"Well," he started, looking back across the street and around the store to be sure no one else would hear, "back at the river crossing, the driver stopped to talk to some folks that had wagons. They was buryin' some men that tried to rob 'em." He put on a smug face and nodded his head, and continued, "The man with the wagons said the outlaws tried to force 'em to pay a toll of a thousand dollars and if they didn't pay, the outlaws was gonna take their women an' anything else they wanted." He nodded firmly, took a deep breath, looked around again and added, "That fella said them outlaws started shootin' and missed, but the fella with the wagons, said his name was Eli, said he didn't! Them folks kilt all them outlaws, buried 'em, and turned the horses loose. That's how come the driver knew it was an outlaw name o' Vaughan, cuz that horse was a purty one, dark sorrel with flaxen mane and tail, four stockings, Mexican saddle with lotsa silver, it was somethin' alright." He nodded again, turned to the side to lean on the counter, and looked at Woodson, "So, you ready to make your order?"

"Nah, don't have 'nuff women in this town that wanna cinch themselves up! Onliest ones that want anythin' else are them three *ladies* o'er to the *Trey of Spades,* and you don't have anything that'd suit them none!"

"Wal, I'm gonna be on that next stage that comes through here tomorrow, so I'll be gone 'fore the sheriff gets back, an' I'm mighty thankful for that. I reckon he'll be some mad when he hears 'bout his cousin!" grumbled the peddler as he put away his catalog and fastened his sample kit. "For now, I'm gonna see if'n any them *ladies* o'er to the *Trey* wanna order any of these goods direct!" He chuckled as he turned away from the counter and started through the door, but stopped dead in his tracks when he saw two men rein up to the hitchrail in front of the sheriff's office and step down. The sun flashed on the badges on their chests and the peddler dropped his kit on the floor as he turned to Woodson, "Yore outhouse out back?" he stammered, holding himself as he hotfooted it through the store room and slapped open the back door.

———

THE WAGONS CROSSED the Willamette River on Skinner's ferry on the south edge of Eugene City, just below the confluence of the Coast fork and the Middle fork of the Willamette. That was late afternoon yesterday, and now they were entering Eli's kind of country, rolling hills covered with pine forests and with the sweet but pungent smell of the wild. He reined up, stood in his stirrups, took a deep breath, eyes closed, and savored the sounds and smells that wafted from the trees. This wasn't the smell of fresh turned soil of the farms, nor the aroma of recently harvested crops, but the scent of wilderness, and he loved it. He had been longing for this since they left Astoria and traveled the river with its mud and silt and debris, the flatlands with farm animals and crops, and the stench of cities. Even the little settlement of Cottage Grove they had just passed had the stench of whiskey, waste, and worse.

But something assaulted his nostrils, and he opened his eyes, felt Rusty fidget beneath him, and heard the snort of the grey as he watched the black and white walking stink of a skunk family parade across the trail in front of him. He lifted the neckerchief to his nose, closed his eyes to the biting stench that made his eyes water and made him cough as he wheeled Rusty around and trotted back down the trail to find some fresh air, even if it was all the way to Cottage Grove, even the whiskey and waste would be less than this! He glanced back to be certain the striped cousin to the felines was not following.

He broke from the trees onto a flat shoulder with a bit of a clearing and reined around, breathing deep of the clear air. He stopped, leaned on his pommel, and looked back up the road to see the wagons coming. He shook his head, looked around, and stepped down, deciding this would be a good spot to stop, give the horses a breather and hopefully let the mountain breeze clear the air. He shook his head, chuckling at how a little creature could bring things to a stop with nothing more than a sashay across the trail. He loosened the girth on his saddle, also the girth on the packsaddle, and led the horses into the shade where some tall grass beckoned.

When the wagons came near, he motioned them off

the roadway and said, "We'll take a short break here, let the horses have a breather, stretch our legs a mite."

With a nod, Anton did as directed, stepped down, and walked to Eli's side. "Trouble?"

Eli grinned, "You might say that, but nothin' too bad. Seems there was another family that had a prior claim on the trail, but they'll be gone soon."

"Prior family?" asked a confused Anton.

Eli chuckled, "Yeah, a black and white family, all of 'em walking slow with their tails in the air and letting the world know they were there."

Anton laughed, returned to his wagon, and helped Freja down to stretch her legs with the other women.

———

THE ROAD KEPT to the east side of the Coast fork of the Willamette River and moved into the timber-covered hills. With less than a half-day behind them since passing Cottage Grove, the trail bent to the west and the river to the east. For the first time in many days, they parted company with the Willamette River and took to the hills. With a steady climb before them, Eli led the way and stretched out his lead as he began his scout for the wagons. There would be times when his reconnoiter would take him further and faster, but today was the first day in the hills and he wanted to stay closer to the wagons, uncertain of how the men and teams would handle the continued climb and the later descent.

Lobo showed the first reaction, but the horses lifted heads and pricked ears and with flared nostrils, tossed their heads and grew skittish. Eli reined up, stood in his stirrups to search the roadway and trees, thinking the skunk family might have returned. The road ahead made an 'S' bend and disappeared into the thick trees. With towering spruce, hemlock, ponderosa, and thicker undergrowth, it was impossible to see anything except the roadway and the first few feet into the woods. But it was evident the horses and Lobo had smelled something, and it was not just the skunk, although the stench of the stinkpot was alarming, it did not cause fear, and it was fear that showed in the eyes and behavior of the horses. Eli backed Rusty down the road, and the free-rein grey stayed right with the claybank. Lobo had dropped into an attack stance, head lowered, hackles standing high, and fangs showing as he let a low growl cut the silence. Lobo looked back to see the horses and Eli backing away, and the wolf, young though he was, showed his smarts as he, too, backed slowly away.

Once they were a good forty yards back down the road, Eli stopped the animals, stepped down and with rifle in hand, moved the horses into the trees and loosely tethered them, tight enough to keep them here, but loose enough to escape if necessary. He motioned to Lobo to come and the two, staying inside the tree line, moved back up the road, searching and watching for any sign of danger.

As he neared the point where the animals first showed alarm, the wolf again dropped his head and raised his hackles, letting another growl rumble from his chest. Eli paused, searched the trees, watching and listening. The snap of jaws and a spit and snarl came from the trees and Eli immediately recognized the sounds as those of a catamount, or cougar. It did not sound like a fight, but rather of a predator feeding on a kill. Eli moved a little deeper into the trees, and with the carpet of pine needles masking his movements, he slowly advanced nearer. The flash of dusky fur and the snarl of a beast tearing at a carcass stopped Eli, who dropped into a crouch and moved slowly side to side to get a better look at the beast.

The big cougar, tail whipping side to side, blood on his chest, face, and paws, was tearing the innards from the body of a black-tail deer. The prey appeared to be a young buck, small antlers clattering against the hard pack of the road as the lion pulled and bit. The scene was at the edge of the road, a definite impediment to any wagons coming through. The presence of a cougar would stampede the teams, none of which would want to go near the beast and would fight their harness and traces, making a wreck of any wagon.

Eli watched as the big catamount took his fill of guts and meat. The cat paused, licking its maw and looking around. He froze, probably picking up the scent of man or wolf. The big cat bent around to look behind him and into the trees, his eyes searching the vicinity of Eli and Lobo. His nostrils flared, his jaw clamped, and his tail moved slowly side to side. The ripples of muscle flickered from his neck to his flank as the cat slowly turned to face in the direction of Eli and the wolf. Suddenly he pawed at the air, split the quiet of the woods with a scream and snarl, mouth wide and bloody face and fangs showing as he snapped his jaws in warning.

Eli dropped to one knee, put his hand on Lobo's scruff and stroked the wolf, whispering, "Easy boy, easy," and watching the lion. With no reaction to his taunt, the big cat turned, grasped the carcass of the deer at the neck, lifted his head to stand tall and straddling the carcass, dragged his prey into the woods. The cat disappeared into the thicker woods, but Eli heard sounds of the dragging for a moment or two, but as the sounds faded, Eli and Lobo relaxed. Eli stood, looked down at

Lobo, "Good boy. That was a close one. That cat would not be fun to tangle with!"

Eli returned to the horses, mounted, slipped the Winchester into the scabbard and nudged Rusty back to the road, and continued his scout.

CHAPTER 17

SOUTH

The men continually proved their worth and experience. Eli was appreciative of their diligence at tending to the animals, harness, wagons, and more. Whenever they stopped, the men routinely checked every working part of harness, running gear, and anything else that might demand attention. An overnight stop saw the men regularly greasing the skein of the axles, the wheel hubs, and bolster plate, the parts of a wagon that continually needed attention, without which they would deteriorate and result in a wagon break-down.

Both the men and women had shown their strength and ability to handle a team and wagon when they took the first run into the hills when the road cut over the long ridge, dropped into a lowland and did a switchback climb to crest the shoulder of another knoll and drop into the long valley that brought them across Bennet and Elk Creeks before turning south after splitting a long ridge and breaking into another long valley. Now they were making camp at the edge of the trees in the shadow of the long ridge, watching the sun drop in the west and make shadows of the distant hills.

Eli had made his usual separate camp and went to the crest of the ridge behind his camp for his systematic reconnoiter of the area. He sat with legs drawn up, elbows on his knees and with binoculars in hand, he searched the land of the dry valley below their camp. There were several dry creeks that came from off the ridge where he sat, and on the far side of the valley, a long finger ridge petered out at the base of a small knoll with scattered juniper freckling the eastern slope, with another long ridge that sided the wagon road and pointed south. The signs of farms and a small settlement showed beyond the knoll, a road coming from there to join the road known as the Oregon-California or Trapper's trail and what some called the Siskiyou trail. Below him, and on the south end of the long ridge where he sat, the hills dropped away with heavy timber and the lighter green of cottonwoods and hardwoods that usually sided creeks. This is what he was looking for, any sign of water that might attract game. It had been a few days since the folks of the wagons had fresh meat and he was hopeful of bagging something that would add to the larder.

With rifle in hand and Lobo at his heels, Eli returned to the camp, mounted the waiting Rusty and with the unburdened pack horse behind, he went after game. Because this was a dry valley, the only farms he saw were on the west side of the wagon road and few of them. Choosing to cross the road because of a promising creek he would later learn was Yoncalla Creek, he spotted movement where the timber fell from the point of another long ridge and joined with the trees that sided the little creek. He reined up and leaned along the neck of the big stallion as they hugged the trees, watching movement on the far side. About a hundred fifty yards away, a sprightly orange and brown long-legged calf bounded into the open, followed close by his drooped neck and big-eared mother, a cow elk. Another cow, probably last year's calf, and without a calf of her own, followed. Two more cows, one with a calf, were pushed from the darker timber by a bull with wide spread antlers and a dark, heavy scruff of a collar.

Eli slowly slipped the Winchester from the scabbard and stepped down. He ground-tied Rusty, motioned for Lobo to stay, and moved closer to the big leaf maple before them. The big tree gave him cover and he dropped to one knee close beside and slightly behind it. He lifted the rifle, sighted in on the bigger lone cow, took a deep breath, let a little out, and slowly squeezed the trigger. The rifle bucked, roared and spat smoke and lead. The bullet flew true, piercing the low chest of the cow, just behind the left front leg and the cow stumbled, tried another step, and dropped to its neck. The alarming blast spooked the rest of the small herd, and they scattered back into the trees in an instant. Eli watched, saw the cow kick once, and silence fell over the woods.

WHEN HE RETURNED to camp with the pack horse loaded and more behind his saddle, he was met with smiling faces and welcome arms as he distributed the meat among the four families, saving a back strap for himself and Candy. Anton stepped close, accepted the offer, and looked at Eli, "You know what today is?"

Eli frowned, "Uh, yeah, it's Friday, I think. Isn't it? Or were you thinking of something else?"

Anton grinned, "No, no. But you should know, we were hoping to be at a settlement when we camp tomorrow, because the following day is the sabbath."

"And you don't want to travel on the sabbath?" asked Eli.

"No, no, that's not it. We were hopeful of finding a church where we could attend and join in the worship."

Eli grinned, "That would be good, and the way I've got it figured, there's two or three settlements we'll come near tomorrow, and we can stop whenever we find something promising. Would that be alright with everyone?

Anton smiled, nodding, and answered, "Oh yes. That would be fine, Eli, fine. Thank you!" He continued nodding as he backstepped, hands full of meat, and turned away to his wagon. It was obvious others were watching and were pleased with his response to Eli's answer.

———

Eli looked at Candy as they rode together ahead of the wagons. They had just passed through what locals called a town, but it was nothing more than one building serving as a general store and tavern combined, with the owner's living quarters behind. It was also connected to a barn that was the livery and blacksmith. One house sat across the street but was empty. There was a sign that said, *Oakland*. Eli chuckled, "Folks seem to think anything that has a store makes it a town."

"Is it that or is it any place with a tavern?" asked Candy. They had crossed Calapooya creek and were still bound south. The trail was taking them through a cut between two buttes. The timber was thick and standing tall as they broke from the buttes and faced a fertile valley with several farms and a few buildings that looked more like a village or a town. Eli glanced to Candy, "Now that looks more like a town, even if there is only this one road, at least there's more'n a store an' a livery."

"But we don't need either one," commented Candy as they kept riding through the little town. A dust devil spun on its nose at the end of the street, a lazy dog lay on the boardwalk of the store, and a pump creaked while someone filled a bucket with water. One man sat on a rocker behind the dog, but neither paid any attention to the two riders.

The road pointed them between two taller timber-covered hills with more hills beyond, both east and west. A green valley opened in the basin between the hills, showing several established farms. The trail cut through another gap between rolling hills and opened into a bigger valley that was bordered on the south, by the meandering North Umpqua River. It was mid-afternoon when they made the crossing of the river, so they pushed on about another five miles until the trail brought them to the north bank of the South Umpqua River, with the town of Roseburgh sitting to the east in a bit of a basin nestled among the hills. Eli looked at Candy, back to the trail and suggested, "Reckon back there," nodding to the north and west, "Back in those thickets where that little creek comes down would be a good place to camp. Then we'll hafta find a church for these folks."

"A church?" asked Candy.

"Yup. They specifically asked to find a church so they could go tomorrow. It *is* Sunday."

"Oh, yeah," grumbled Candy as he nudged Sundowner to the trees to make their camp.

The two had finished stripping the horses of the gear, picketed them near the little stream with ample grass, rolled out their sougans and set up their cookfire. Eli had grabbed the coffee pot and started for the stream when he heard the commotion of the arriving wagons. Candy waved him off and walked from the trees to greet the wagons and, of course, the girls, grinning as they approached and called out to him.

The two were invited to share supper with the group who had planned on a Saturday night feast, with each family preparing something different to make a smorgasbord for everyone. When everyone had their plates full and went to their places—the adults around the makeshift table and the youngsters scattered about on blankets and boxes—Anton stood and with a nod to Marcus Moller, "Let's have Marcus ask the Lord's blessing on our meal."

Marcus gave a brief prayer of thanksgiving and concluded with an "Amen," which was echoed by everyone, and the conversation began to roll as they partook of the bounty. The wagons were parked in their usual horseshoe shape formation, with the table in the bend of the shape. It was a pleasant time and there was ample laughter and flirting on the part of the two older girls and Candy, who just happened to be sitting near one another.

As they were finishing the meal, Olivia Hansen announced, "We have a special desert! Cake with a fresh fruit compote made of chokecherries, service berries, and gooseberries." She giggled as she and Alma Pedersen went to the back of the Pedersen wagon to retrieve the desert. The women started passing filled bowls around to everyone and each was excited about the rare desert when the party was rudely interrupted when a rider came into the opening of the formation, riding hard and reining his mount to a sliding stop, causing a considerable dust cloud to settle over the table and all the fixings.

"Yeah, just as I thought! You're the bunch alright!" growled the rider. He sat atop a flashy tall horse with similar color and marking to that used by the outlaws that tried to extort the wagons of a toll. Eli immediately thought of the outlaw and the idea given by the stage driver that the outlaw's cousin was the sheriff of Linn County. The man sat with his rifle over the saddle bow and pointed toward the people at the table.

"Here, here, what is this?" demanded Anton Lund as he stood at the head of the table and faced the intruder. "What do you mean riding in here like that and pointing that rifle at us?"

The rider growled, "Just you sit down 'fore I use this hyar rifle, startin' with you!"

The man grabbed the edge of his jacket and pulled it back to reveal a tin star pinned to his chest. "I'm Sheriff Harvey Smith. I'm the sheriff o'er to Albany in Linn county where you and your bunch killed five men and I'm lookin' for a man name o' Eli! Now which one o' you is Eli?" he demanded, lifting his rifle and pointing the muzzle at the crowd, moving it side to side. "Which one o' you kilt muh cousin?"

The two boys, Lucas Pedersen and Soren Moller, were seated on a long box, intently watching the sheriff, and when he asked, Lucas stood and pointed at Eli, "He done it! An' he saved the girls when he done it too!"

"Yeah, they was gonna take the girls!" added Soren,

and not to be outdone, he pointed to Candy, "An' he helped!"

"Boys! Sit down and be quiet!" demanded Anton, looking from the boys back to the sheriff.

The sheriff was grinning and glared at Eli, "So you shot down muh cousin, didja?" he growled. "So, now I'm gonna take you back to Albany so we can hang you!"

"Now, hold on there, sheriff. The boys are right, the outlaws were demanding us to pay them a thousand dollars and threatened to take our women and everything else if we didn't pay up. Then Eli," nodding to Eli, who stood at the corner of the table facing the sheriff, "told them they couldn't, they turned and started shooting. There was nothing else we could do but fight back!" responded Anton.

Erik Pedersen stood and added, "That's right, sheriff. If he hadn't returned fire, those men would have killed him and the rest of us, then taken everything else, they said so!"

"Yeah, well they didn't kill anybody, and you done kilt all o' them so they can't tell the truth of the matter. That's why I'm takin' him, an' you," pointing his rifle at Candy, "back with me!"

Eli stepped forward, "Now, hold on, sheriff. Before we act too hasty, there's something you might consider. Suppose, just suppose, that after we had the run-in with your cousin and his outlaw friends, we went to see Sheriff Joe Meador of Lane County and told him about what happened. Now you can just picture sheriff Joe scratching his beard, looking at us, and telling us about you. But then he might have added, 'Since that happened in Linn County, Sheriff Smith might wanna come huntin' you, but he has no authority here in Lane County, and based on what you told me, you folks done nothin' wrong,' and he sent us on our way."

"Don't care what Meador says, it happened in my county, and that's where I'm takin' you!" growled the angry sheriff.

Eli stepped a little closer, held up one hand, and continued, "And just suppose we went into Roseburgh and talked to Sheriff Elijah Livingston and told him the same thing. Now you know Sheriff Livingston would say the same thing as the sheriff of Lane County. We did nothing wrong but defend ourselves from some outlaws, and besides that, can't you just hear him saying, 'we're in Douglas County, and even if Sheriff Smith is cousins with the leader of the gang, which by the way, we've been huntin' him for some time now and you saved us a lotta trouble, that doesn't make any difference, because Sheriff Smith has no jurisdiction in Douglas County.'"

Eli crossed his arms over his chest, looked at the sheriff, "Now, Sheriff, do you really want to go against two other sheriff's seein' as how you're outta your jurisdiction and have no legal authority to take anybody?"

The sheriff growled and brought the rifle around to point directly at Eli, "Now you listen here! I don't give two hoots about jurisdiction. The way I see it, this is a personal matter and we're gonna take you two in, no matter what!"

"We?" asked Eli, frowning at the sheriff.

"Yes, we!" he growled, lifting his chin to point at the opening between the wagons where two other men stood behind everyone, both holding rifles at the ready.

Eli looked about and saw the three men had the entire group in a crossfire and if they did anything to resist, there would be deadly consequences, and innocent people could be killed. He glanced to Candy, who gave a slight nod, and turned back to face the sheriff. "Alright, sheriff, we'll go with you. Just have your men come with us to our camp so we can get our horses and gear."

With a nod and a wave of his rifle, the sheriff motioned for the two to go with Eli and Candy, "But drop your pistols on the table right there first," he growled.

CHAPTER 18

DELIVERANCE

Both Eli and Candy opened their jackets wide and slipped their pistols from the holsters, and lay them on the corner of the table. With a nod from the sheriff, they turned and started to their camp to retrieve their horses. As they moved away, the sheriff called after them, "And just in case you try anything stupid, just remember I've got my rifle on the rest of these bumpkins." He laughed as he looked at the rest of the people, some standing, others seated, the women trying to control the children.

The sheriff was a big man who looked even bigger aboard his horse that stood a good sixteen hands. He sneered at the people around the table, grumbling all the while. He scratched his beard with his free hand, pushed the felt hat back on his head to scratch his thinning hair, and shifted his weight in the saddle, looking for some comfort while he waited. His wool jacket hung loosely over his big frame and his high topped boots had big rowel spurs he kept jabbing into the ribs of his fidgety horse.

The two deputies demanded Eli and Candy lock their fingers behind their head as they walked up the slight rise to their camp in the trees. One man, a bit slovenly with patchy whiskers that hadn't seen a razor for at least a week, a leather vest over a homespun shirt and whip-cord britches, was the more dominant of the two and gave the orders to the other. The second man, about the same size at just shy of six feet, twelve and a half stone, deep-chested and burly, but quiet in demeanor.

When the first man ordered, "Gus, you stay with 'em, I'll check their gear."

Gus responded, "Who made you the boss, Cecil?"

"Oh, just do it! You don' wanna have 'em come up with another weapon, do ya?" grunted Cecil, lowering his rifle as he walked past Eli and Candy, going to their packs and gear.

"Nah, go 'head on, do it!" answered Gus.

The gear was stacked under a wide-spreading hemlock, and the horses were tethered on either side. For Cecil to go to the gear, he was between the horses and Eli knew they needed to have the men separated if they were going to try to break free. He nodded to Candy, who started to his Criollo stallion, and Eli started toward his claybank. Gus followed close to Eli, but Candy drew near to Cecil as he reached for his saddle that lay between the horse and the other gear. He saw Cecil moving the gear around and knew he would see the Spencer and Colt shotgun once the pack saddle was lifted. Earlier, when Candy was told to put his pistol on the table, he intentionally turned a little sideways when he opened his jacket to lift the pistol from his left hip holster and placed it on the table, but his second pistol was obscured by the loose fold of his bolero jacket. As he bent to pick up his saddle, he slipped the pistol from the holster with his left hand as he grabbed the saddle with his right.

Cecil saw Candy lift the saddle, saw the rifle in the scabbard, and called out, "Hold it! Let me have that rifle!" he demanded, stepping close to Candy with the saddle between them. He reached for the stock of the rifle, and Candy dropped the saddle, stood with his pistol pointed at Cecil's face, and spoke softly, "Now you drop your rifle, señor!"

The movement caught the attention of Gus, who turned, swinging his rifle toward Candy, but Eli snatched the LeMat from the holster at his back and brought it around in a swinging arc to club Gus above the ear and drop him unconscious to the ground in a heap.

Candy ordered Cecil, who had dropped his rifle and lifted his hands, "Now you back away, slowly, señor," and followed him, the pistol held before him.

"So, Eli, what do we do with him now?"

"Sit him down and bind his hands behind his back, put a rag in his mouth too," directed Eli, "Let me think about this." He holstered his pistol and dragged the unconscious Gus to where Candy had tied Cecil to the tree, gagged and bound. Eli did the same with Gus, stood and looked at the two, glanced to Candy.

"Here's what I think might work." He dropped to a crouch to look under the wide-spread branches of the trees toward the wagons. The wagons were between them and the people at the table, now held hostage by the sheriff, and Eli began to explain his plan to Candy, who chuckled as he heard Eli's idea.

"Si, I think it will work. You give me a moment to sneak back behind the wagons, then you take off. I'll keep the sheriff from harming the others."

"Good, good," declared a grinning Eli, who hurriedly

began saddling Rusty. When he was ready, he grabbed the Colt shotgun from the pack, lay it across the saddle bow, and swung aboard the big stallion. With a nod to Candy, he watched the Charro slip from the camp and move to the wagons in a crouch. The sun had dropped behind the west horizon, but the light of dusk covered the land while the shadows were gathering in the trees and elsewhere. A few moments later, Eli turned Rusty to the edge of the trees, reached down to stroke his neck. "Alright, boy, we've got 'er to do!" He sat up, slapped legs to the stallion and the pair lunged from the trees, the big claybank stretched into an all-out run as they broke into the open. He hollered back over his shoulder as if he were escaping and lay low on the neck of Rusty, slapping legs to his sides to encourage him on. With a glance to the wagons, he saw the sheriff lift his rifle as he turned, heard the bark of the weapon, heard the whistle of the bullet, and knew he was in the clear.

The sheriff dug spurs into the ribs of his mount as he jerked the head of the horse around and gave chase to Eli. Those at the table jumped to their feet, watching the two riders disappear in the dust. The wagons were camped in a basin below a slightly bald peak that marked the end of a long timber-covered ridge that nosed into the bend of the South Umpqua River. When Eli rode from the basin, he was headed due west into the gold-glowing sky that remained from the setting sun. He lay low on the neck of Rusty, confident that no horse could catch the long-legged stallion, but Eli was determined—not to escape—to lead the sheriff away from the wagons before confronting him.

Eli swung Rusty around the point of a finger ridge and turned back into the long draw between the ridges that pointed back to the eastern mountains. He pushed

Rusty into the trees, swung down, shotgun in hand, and dropped to a crouch, waiting for the sheriff. The thunder of hooves on the grassy flat told of the approach of the sheriff, and Eli slipped his LeMat from the holster, stepped into the open and fired a round over the head of the sheriff, prompting the man to bring his horse to a stop. Eli slipped the LeMat behind his belt and lifted the Colt as he watched the sheriff swing down and slap the rump of his horse to get him away. The sheriff brought his rifle up as the horse kicked clods of dirt, getting away.

"Don't do it, sheriff!" warned Eli. But the vengeful sheriff with hate-filled eyes glared at Eli and lifted the rifle. Before he could bring it level, the Colt boomed, kicking back to jolt Eli, but the fist full of ten gauge double-aught pellets cut through the air and made mincemeat of the right hand, arm, and shoulder of the sheriff, making him drop his rifle and stagger backward. He stumbled, fell to his back, and rolled to his side, whimpering and crying, "You kilt me! You kilt me!"

Eli walked to the man, the shotgun held before him, and said, "You aren't killed, but you are a mess. You look like a flock of buzzards were making supper outta you! But, if you want more..." he ratcheted the cylinder on the shotgun by cocking the hammer. The clatter of metal on metal brought the sheriff wide-eyed and trying to get away by kicking with his feet and sliding on his back, "NO! NO!" he cried, holding out his uninjured hand as if it would protect him from another blast from the shotgun.

Eli stepped closer, dropped to his heels beside the sheriff, and said, "You need to have that looked at, sheriff." He reached down and slipped the pistol from the holster on the man's hip, flipped open his jacket to see if he had any other weapons, and, seeing a sheathed knife, slipped it out and lay it beside the pistol. "Anything else, sheriff?"

"No, no, nuthin'," whimpered the man. "Help me, I need a doctor!"

Eli stepped back, "Stand up, we'll get the horses, and I'll see what we can do for you," he explained.

As they rode back into the wagon camp, he called out to the others, "Could a couple you ladies get me some rags we can use to bandage this man up 'fore he bleeds to death?" All the ladies scampered to their wagons and soon returned to the table where Eli had gotten the sheriff and sat him down. He looked to one of the wagons and saw the other two deputies tied and bound to the wagon wheels and he grinned at Candy, "I see you handled those two alright."

"Ah, no problem, amigo," he answered, chuckling.

CHAPTER 19

HIGH COUNTRY

With a full moon, the families decided to continue their journey and put Roseburgh behind them. After leaving the sheriff at the doctor's office and the deputies at the jail, they made another fifteen miles before making camp and taking the day off from traveling. The trail kept to the east side of the Umpqua River—where ash, cottonwood, and dogwood were proliferate—while on the semi-bald slopes that climbed the higher hills on the east side, juniper, larch and cedar were scattered. They found a bit of a basin where a little creek met with the river and the wagons pulled off the road to make camp. The big moon shone bright, but the dim light challenged the travelers as they settled in for the rest of the night. With no church nearby, they decided their own lay pastor, Marcus Moller, would preach, and they would have their own church service, howbeit a little later than expected.

It was late morning when the families dragged themselves from their bedrolls. The women started whipping up the morning meal while the menfolk gathered firewood and started the cookfires. With the women busy making breakfast, the men tended the stock, giving all the horses a good rub-down, leading them to water, and picketed them on good graze. Eli and Candy came from their camp just inside the trees, standing and arching their back and stretching their arms to the sky. Eli looked about and said, "Looks to be a nice day!"

Candy looked at Eli, shook his head, "Depends on breakfast," grumbled the still-sleepy Candy.

The men were busy arranging seating for the church service, allowing the youngsters and others to take their breakfast to the seats and begin eating. Marcus Moller was preparing a makeshift pulpit, stopping often to partake of his coffee and flip through pages of his Bible. Eli and Candy found a shady spot beside one of the wagons and sat, legs stretched out and their hats hanging on the hub of a wheel, their plates in their laps, and began enjoying the unique breakfast of *weinerbrød* or pastry with a sausage and soft cheese. Both men, who thought themselves quite hungry, had asked for and received a second helping, and had *håndværkere,* a croissant with soft cheese and fruit compote. Both had a soft-boiled egg that sat beside the rest as if waiting its turn.

The rattle of trace chains and the shout of a jehu caught their attention and both Eli and Candy rose to their feet to see a stagecoach chased by a dust cloud as it rounded the bend in the road. The jehu saw the gathering of wagons, leaned back to pull on the lines and bring the coach to a stop. Once the dust cloud had passed them by, the driver called out, "Looks like you folks are getting ready for church, that right?"

Eli chuckled, walked a bit closer and answered, "That's right. These fine folks are pretty insistent on taking time out on the Lord's day and having a time of worship," motioning with a wave of his hand behind him to the others who were watching as he spoke with the driver.

"Wal, that's wonderful. Say, would you mind if we's joined you? I've got some folks aboard that were snivelin' 'bout missin' church and I promised 'em that if we ran onto one, we'd stop. Now, I didn't rightly think that'd happen, but..." he shrugged and grinned as he leaned toward Eli.

Eli turned and called out to Marcus, "Hey, Parson! Alright if these folks join in?"

"Why, of course, and welcome," answered the big, broad-shouldered Dane. He stood behind his makeshift pulpit, Bible in hand, and motioned them to join.

With a nod, the Jehu reined the six-up off the roadway, stopped, and with a nod to the messenger, who responded by climbing down, opening the coach door, and announcing, "Wal folks, church is about to start. Come on down if'n you're of a mind." He stepped back to make way, and the coach spilled out its passengers.

First out was a woman who was gaily attired with a grey crinoline skirt, lace and brocade across the bodice and neckline, a matching bonnet, parasol, and reticule. Her lace-up high-topped shoes showed a taller-than-usual heel. She was followed by a gentleman in a dark wool suit with a lounge jacket, matching waistcoat, and striped trousers. He carried a beaver top hat which he put on as he exited the coach, taking the time to look about and to look down at all the lesser peoples around. He huffed, stepped down, offered his arm to the lady and they walked side by side to the gathering.

Five other passengers followed. Two looked like cowboys with leather vests, floppy felt hats, and sidearms. The other two men were non-descript, having the appearance of settlers or farmers. A lone woman with a plain blue crinoline cotton dress with a tall collar and little decoration. She had a bonnet of pale yellow and a reticule hanging from her wrist. She stepped down, glancing about, and dropped her eyes as she followed the others to the seats and benches added by the families of the wagons who made way for all the visitors.

As the people settled into their places, Eli was surprised to see the older of the youngsters, Asta Hansen with an accordion, Emilie Lund with a wooden flute, Niels Pedersen with a fiddle, and Lucas Pedersen with a mouth harp. They walked to the front and as Marcus Moller directed, they began playing *There's a Wideness in God's Mercy*, and everyone began singing.

> *There's a wideness in God's mercy, Like the wide-*
>   *ness of the sea;*
> *There's a kindness in God's justice, Which is more*
>   *than liberty.*
> *There is welcome for the sinner, and more graces*
>   *for the good;*
> *There is mercy with the Savior, There is healing in*
>   *His blood.*

They continued for two more verses, and with a brief pause, Marcus began another hymn, *Revive Us Again*. Everyone joined in, whether they had a singing voice or not, but their enthusiasm seemed to overcome their lack.

> *We praise Thee, O God! For the Son of Thy Love,*
> *For Jesus, Who died and is now gone above.*
> *Hallelujah! Thine the glory. Hallelujah! Amen.*
> *Hallelujah! Thine the glory, Revive us again.*

This song also continued for three more verses, and most were content to listen to the instruments rather than try to keep up with words they did not know. As the song ended, the pastor stepped forward, thanked the musicians, and turned to the crowd.

"This morning, I would like to take my text from the book of Ephesians, chapter 2, verses 8 and 9. *For by grace are ye saved through faith; and that not of yourselves: it is the gift of God: Not of works, lest any man should boast.*

He set his Bible aside and began, "I want to focus on three words: Grace, Saved, and Faith. First, Grace—that's when God, in His goodness, kinda overlooks some of the things we do. I often think of my father and the times I probably should have gotten a whipping, but my father would sit down and explain to me what I should have done, and because of his grace, I did not get a whipping. That's what I mean. In our lives, there are times I am certain that God watches, shakes his head, and takes a deep breath, and because of His grace, we don't get the whipping we deserve.

And the second word is Saved. Just like when my father talked to me, I was saved or spared from that whipping. When God's Word talks about Saved, He's talking about salvation—being saved from what we deserve because of our sin—which is Hell forever. But because of His grace, He sent His Son, Jesus, to pay the price for our sin so we would not have to, and we were saved from that horrible end.

And then Faith—faith is nothing more than believing God. When he says the penalty for sin is death—that's the death and hell forever kind of penalty—then we should believe Him. That's faith. And when he says Jesus paid the penalty, we believe it. That's faith. And when he says *it is the gift of God, not of works,* we believe it. That's faith. But too many times, we think to get to Heaven, we have to work it out!"

The pastor shook his head, chuckling as he stepped beside the pulpit, and with one arm on the pulpit, he looked at the people, "Now, I ask you. If we have to work for it, how much work would we have to do? And if we can lose it just as easy, is it because of one sin, many sins, or..." he shrugged, returned behind the pulpit. "That's why the rest of our verse says, *Not of works, lest any man should boast.* See, if it was because of my good works, then each of us would be struttin' around heaven braggin' 'bout what we done! And Heaven is no place for braggarts!

So, it's by faith, that's believing God, knowing that because of His grace, not getting what we deserve, we can have that gift of eternal life. And to get that gift, according to Romans 10, all we have to do is ask. So, my friends, has there been a time in your life that you have asked God for the gift of eternal life? If not, you can do that today, or anytime, just ask Him for it. It's that simple, and when you do, hold on, He'll change your life!"

The pastor grinned, bowed his head, and closed in prayer. At the conclusion of the prayer, he looked up at everyone and added, "Folks, the ladies have asked me to announce that everyone is invited to stay for lunch!"

The jehu and messenger had joined Eli and Candy to stand and lean against the wagons as the pastor delivered his message, and at the invitation, the driver turned to Eli, "Now that's the kind of invitation I like!"

CHAPTER 20

PASSES

"When I was talking with the driver and messenger with the stage, you know, while you were flirting with the girls," chuckled Eli as he and Candy rode side-by-side on the trail as it dropped to the low hills to cross the wide park between the bigger ridges, "they said there's been some of the Cow Creek Band of Umpqua that have been hittin' some travelers in the mountains yonder," pointing to the mountains before them with his chin. They had crossed the South Umpqua River earlier this morning and were now taking the trail that left the river bottom to move into the higher hill country.

The trail sided Canyon Creek and pushed into the canyon that split the rugged, steep mountains that showed broad shoulders of basaltic outcroppings and heavy timber that climbed the steep slopes. The mountains pushed in on the little creek that chuckled and giggled through the thickets of alder and willow, never more than a few feet wide and less than a foot deep, it carried crystal clear and ice-cold water. Fed by mountain springs that harbored deep wells of snow melt, the little stream pushed its way through the formidable mountains, laughing all the way.

With a steady pull all the way, the trail would climb another fifteen hundred feet before topping out to drop into another long canyon. The mountains on either side would stand tall another fifteen hundred feet higher, or about thirty-five hundred feet, giving them a lofty overlook for the broad expanse of southern Oregon and northern California. They were in rough country, and there would be little forgiveness for any mistakes, either by beast or wagons.

Eli and Candy rode about a mile or more ahead of the wagons, and as they neared the confluence of a little fork that came from the west and merged with Canyon Creek, they spooked a trio of black-tail deer. Eli snatched his Winchester from the scabbard, took a quick aim, and fired. His targeted buck stumbled, fell, and rolled into the creek as the other two disappeared into the trees. Candy laughed, "When you grabbed that rifle, I thought we were in trouble, but you were just getting meat!"

"Yup. Can't pass up an opportunity like that!" replied Eli, slipping the Winchester back into the scabbard and using knee pressure to move Rusty toward the downed carcass. Eli looked at Candy, "Well, you gonna help?"

Candy chuckled, "Si, señor, si. Candy will help you," he answered as he stepped down, ground tying his mount and slipping his knife from the scabbard. They dragged the buck from the creek, rolled it to its back, and Eli cut him from tail to chin to split the hide open and begin their work. As they worked, Candy asked, "That man yesterday, you know, what he said, do you believe that?"

Eli frowned, "You mean the preacher?"

"Si, the pastor. You know, when he said you don't work for salvation, it is a gift. Is that right?"

"Yes, it is. That's what the Bible says, like he said, *not of works, lest any man should boast.*"

"So, how do we get this gift?" asked Candy, trying to be nonchalant in his manner, looking at his knife work rather than Eli.

"Just ask, you know, in prayer, we ask for God's forgiveness, ask for His free gift of salvation, and He will give it."

"But, what about church, confession, rosary, you know," questioned Candy, glancing to Eli.

"Those are works, the things we do, and it has nothing to do with the free gift of salvation. However, once we receive that gift, then we want to do whatever He wants us to, but it's easier then," explained Eli.

"Have you done that? Receive the gift, I mean."

"Yes, I have. And since that time, I want to do more for Him. I read my Bible regularly, spend time in prayer with Him, do what good I can, you know, live for Him," clarified Eli.

"How do I do that?" casually remarked Candy.

"In prayer. If you would like, we can pray together, and I'll lead you."

Candy stopped what he was doing, wiped his bloody hands on the carcass of the deer, sat back, and looked at Eli. "Yes, I would like that. I need to know that I have salvation and that I will go to Heaven."

Eli wiped his hands, laid his knife aside, and sat down on the grass, pulled his knees up, and with elbows on his knees, he looked at Candy, "Let's pray,"

The men prayed together, Eli leading as he gave him the simple words to ask forgiveness, ask for the free gift of salvation paid for by Jesus on the cross, and for strength to walk the Christian life. Eli closed with an "Amen" that was echoed by Candy, and the men shook hands, breathed a deep sigh of relief, and quickly finished their work on the meat.

With the deboned meat wrapped in the hide of the deer, two bundles were hung on the packsaddle of the grey, whose load had been lightened by transferring much of the gear to the wagons. They no sooner mounted up, when a glance down the road showed the wagons nearing. Eli looked to the sun, back to the wagons, chuckled to Candy, "Reckon this'll be as good a place as any for our noonin'!"

———

THE STEADY CLIMB continued for several days, although the country they were passing through was rugged, timbered, and beautiful, the constant climb and drop over the rough hills was wearing on both the animals and equipment. They camped near Cow Creek before assaulting another climb into the mountains and were accosted by a small band of Cow Creek Umpqua natives, but they showed no hostility. They just needed food and were willing to trade, but the Danes were willing to share what they had, and the band of what some would call renegades eagerly accepted the offerings and left peacefully.

After leaving Cow Creek and taking to the mountains again, they passed Rattlesnake Creek, Wolf Creek, and Coyote Creek and made another long climb before dropping into the Salmon Creek valley. But the easy road gave way to another climb, crossing of Jumpoff Joe creek and crossing a valley where several established farms dotted the flats, all claimed with the Donation Land Act. After another mountain crossing, the trail sided the Rogue River they followed for another long day before parting company with the Rogue and turning south. They bypassed Jacksonville and pushed on to Ashland, where they decided to take a day off from traveling and get some repair work done to the wagons. The smithy was also a good wheelwright, and they needed his work.

Ashland was a bustling town, snuggled up to the bosom of the Siskiyou Mountains foothills, but these mountains were bigger and more rugged than what they had already traversed. These foothills rose to four, five thousand feet and higher, and the Cascade Range was shouldering closer to their trail. As they neared the town, a circuit-riding preacher of the United Methodist faith rode up beside them, greeted them and explained he was a preacher of the gospel and would be holding services in town and invited them to join. Anton grinned, looked at the others, and answered, "We would be happy to join you, pastor."

"Then we'll see you in the morning!" He declared, gave them the location of the home where the families were meeting, turned off from the trail, and waved as he left. It was early afternoon and they pulled up at the livery and blacksmith where Eli waited, and after the greetings and explanations, two wagons were left at the livery. The other two, with everyone together, retreated to Bear Creek to make camp.

Come morning, Eli and Candy chose to go into town, go to a café and visit with some locals to get some information on the upcoming Siskiyou pass. They rose early and slipped out of camp before the rest of the families stirred. The downtown was busier than expected, especially for a Sunday morning, but it appeared that most considered it to be another business day. The Corner

Café appeared to be busy, but looking through the window, they spotted an empty table and eagerly made their way in and settled at the table to be greeted by an attractive woman of mid-twenties who smiled and welcomed them, "And what can I get for you boys?" she asked as she poured their cups full of steaming coffee.

They ordered the 'special', and she brought out two heaping plates with steaks, eggs, bacon, fried potatoes, biscuits, and gravy. Candy laughed, "This sure beats those little sandwiches those folks been fixin'!"

Eli grinned, chuckled, and after a brief prayer, started in on the morning feast. When the waitress returned with more coffee, they asked if there was anyone that could give them some information on the pass. She grinned, nodding, "The best one is Cooky. He used to haul freight o'er the pass real reg'lar until he lost his toes to frostbite. I'll tell him to join you for some coffee as soon as he can, you just sit comfortable till then." She smiled and turned away to return to the kitchen.

The crowd thinned, and as most folks were sitting over cups of coffee, a pot-bellied apron-covered and bald-headed red nose came through the swinging door from the kitchen, grinned with a chuckle, and waddled over to the table. "Howdy, boys! Reckon you be the ones what wanna know all 'bout the Siskiyou?"

Eli chuckled, motioned to the empty chair, and welcomed Cooky with a handshake as he introduced himself and Candy. "That's right. You must be Cooky!"

"Tha's me! Been o'er that pass more time than I can recomember!" he declared as he seated himself. "If I don't know it, ain't nobody knows it!"

And he was true to his word as he gave them a mile-by-mile account of every turn, climb, narrows, and more of the mountain pass. "You climb near'bouts twenty-five hunnert feet, mebbe more, from here to the top. It's a hard pull too, I'd recommend you get some extry horses to help pull them wagons to the top. The livery there has a feller that'd go with you, bring the horses back after yore done wit' 'em."

Eli glanced to Candy, looked to Cooky, "That sounds like good advice to me, Cooky, and we're certainly thankful for your help. We'll be headin' out in the morning, hope to make the crest 'bout early to mid-afternoon."

"You'll be lucky to make it 'fore dark, but there's springs up there, so you won't go without water if'n you hafta camp."

Eli stood, as did Candy, and extended his hand to shake with Cooky, "Thank you for your help. We'll be talkin' to the livery, see if we can get those extra horses too. Thanks again, Cooky."

"Yore entirely welcome, and I hope you make it without any problems," he declared as he also rose, cup in hand, to return to his kitchen. "See ya!" he declared with a wave over his shoulder.

CHAPTER 21

SISKIYOU

They sat around the campfire after their noon meal, enjoying the time of relaxing and rest. Eli began explaining to the men of the wagons about the trail ahead, "The man we talked to used to drive freighters over the pass, been over it several times, and gave a turn-by-turn description. He said in the next about fifteen miles, that trail climbs to over forty-five hundred feet, making it a climb of about twenty-five hundred feet uphill from here. He said the livery here hires out extra teams to help make the climb, and he thought it would be best for us to use them."

Eli reached for the coffee pot and refilled his cup, sat back on the bench, and looked around at the men. He was surprised to see them grinning and chuckling to one another until Anton looked at Eli, "Our horses have not even had a good pull yet. These are Jutland horses, the horses of the Vikings!"

"Vikings?! But—" began Eli and was interrupted by Anton, who was grinning and scooted to the edge of his seat, both hands holding his coffee between his knees.

"These are the horses we will breed. They have a long line of good breeding. Our forefathers bred some with Belgian and Suffolk Punch, but our fathers brought a stud and three mares from the old country when they came to America, and they also found some that were from Nova Scotia that we believe were direct descendants from the Vikings. These are bred to pull, and they have not had a challenge yet. We do not need others." He looked at the other men, who were grinning and nodding their agreement. "Every wagon has harness for two teams, although we have only used one team so far, we will double up as we make this climb, and you will see what great teams they are!"

"Well, I'll have to take your word for it. Up until now, I paid little attention to the horses, although I do like the coloring on most of them. That chestnut with the light mane is a good look. But to be honest, I just thought they were typical plow horses that most settlers bring out."

The expression on the men's faces was common, and all appeared insulted and disappointed at the comparison with plow horses, and they looked at one another, shaking their heads at the remark. Eli noticed their response and quickly added, "Now, I didn't mean anything wrong with that. The problem is not your horses, it's my lack of understanding. You see, my wife's family has a horse breeding farm in Kentucky, and they have some fine horses, Thoroughbreds, Morgans, Arabians, and more. My horse, Rusty, is a cross between a Tennessee Walker and a Morgan, and Candy's horse is a Criollo, an ancient breed from Argentina. But as you can tell, we don't know much about draft horses."

Erik Pedersen added, "And you both have fine horses, but ours are working horses and need to have the size and muscle that gives them that big look. Most of the Jutland horses will be about sixteen to eighteen hundred pounds and about sixteen hands tall."

Candy added, "Both our horses are about sixteen hands also, but they do not have the bulk of your horses. I am anxious to see them pull tomorrow."

They continued with their coffee-drinking and talking, covering most topics of the trail until Candy noticed Eli with a folded newspaper tucked under his leg. He nodded to the paper and asked, "Something interesting happening in the world we don't know about?"

Eli chuckled, pulled the paper from under his leg and glanced at it, "You know, I've pretty well read this through, and everything still seems to be about the same, all the politicians are still arguing about state's rights, civil rights, and impeaching the president. But I did find something interesting that was a little different," he unfolded the paper, pointed to the article, and handed it to Candy, "Read that."

Everyone sat silent while Candy read, watching his facial expressions change from disgust to surprise and more. He shook his head as he handed it back to Eli, but Leif Hansen asked, "So, what was so interesting?" glancing from Eli to Candy.

Eli chuckled and looked to Candy. "You tell 'em!"

Candy shook his head and looked at the men, "Some people will do anything for money! From what that said," nodding to the paper in Eli's hands, "two young people, a brother and sister, heard about someone going into the sewers of New York and looking for lost jewelry and other valuables. He came out after a few days with $27,000 worth of stuff." He paused, shaking his head as the other men frowned, wondering if it was true, "And the two young people, the girl eighteen and the boy sixteen, planned to do the same thing. They spent two weeks in the sewer, had several bags and brought up their findings several times, went back down, and after the two weeks in the sewer, they had $1,500,000 worth of jewelry and more."

The men leaned forward, looked at one another, then at Candy and Eli, "Is that true?" asked Leif. He looked at the other men, "That sounds the same as someone diving into a two-hole outhouse, head first!" The others laughed, shook their heads, and looked at Eli.

"That's what the paper says," began Eli. Says here," pointing at the article, "One ring was worth $16,000, two more at $5,000, and one at $3,000. It says after they got cleaned up, the rich young people headed for England!" he laughed as he folded the paper. "My dad always said that when it comes to money, some people will do anything. I thought I'd seen and heard of every-thing, but nothing like this!" He slapped at the news-paper with his knuckles, "I'm keeping this just to remind me people will do anything for money!"

After getting the repaired wagons from the livery, the men did a double hook-up on each of the wagons, and with broad grins, they nodded when Eli motioned for them to move out. Whips cracked over the teams, wagons groaned and creaked, trace chains rattled as they drew taut, the big horses leaned into their collars and the wagons took to the trail. Eli stretched out Rusty and took the lead by about a mile but was brought up when he heard the mutter of distant thunder. Dark clouds were building beyond the crest of the pass, and he glimpsed jagged silver swords pierce the clouds and drive into the ground. He counted off the seconds and judged the storm to be well on the far side of the crest, yet it appeared to be crawling up the mountains and drawing nearer.

Eli reined around and rode back to the lead wagon, driven by Erik Pedersen, and motioned to the distant storm, "That'll hit us prob'ly before we top out," as he talked, he was loosening his new Mackintosh raincoat from his bedroll and shrugged into it, "if you can pick up the pace, might help us."

The wind was picking up and howling off the steep slopes, rattling the branches of the trees below them and all about them. The road had taken to the shoulders of the hills that stood tall and proud on the west, the wide park with the many runoff creeks that came from the hills on both sides held the scraggly cottonwoods, elm, alder and willows below them. The east side of the park showed the long finger ridges that clawed their way from the foothills to scratch at the bottom land of the park. While in the distance, the towering peaks of the Cascade Range scraped the remnants of blue sky. Lesser mountains rose to the west and south, where the Siskiyou Range of mountains marched along the border between Oregon and California.

Eli had no more stretched out Rusty than the mutter of thunder rolled before them, and the dark clouds sheathed the skeletal fingers of white lightning. The clatter and roar of the elements told of the nearness of the storm and Eli pulled the coat closed across his chest, jerked his hat down tight, and tucked his chin into his collar as he leaned into the cold, wet wind that began its blast as it rose over the crest of the hills before him.

The black timber that stood unrelenting on both sides of the road offered little protection as the fingers of the storm traced their way along the road as if feeling for prey. But the sway of the big spruce and pine was somehow comforting to Eli. Lobo had been staying close beside the big claybank, often between the stallion and the grey packhorse, but continually warily watched the woods and the road.

The rain came like a shaken-out sheet, big drops merciless as they pelted the travelers with cold and a fierceness that sought to turn them away. But neither Eli nor the others gave thought to anything but continuing. Even though the hardpacked road began to give way, muck and mud held the water turning the trail into a quagmire. Rusty began high stepping, lifting mud-packed hooves above the mess, picking each step with caution. Eli could feel each time a hoof slipped, did his best to help the horse keep his footing, glanced at the packhorse that was also tenuous in his steps.

Eli shaded his eyes with his hand and saw something across the road. His first thought was a felled tree, but it was different, bigger. As they neared, slipping and slid-ing, he saw a stagecoach, rear wheels hanging off the drop-off on the east edge of the road, the six up of horses stretched across the road, struggling with the harness and footing, the two leaders were down, tossing their heads, trying to rise, but unable. The driver and messenger were atop, the driver cracking his whip, hollering encouragement to the horses, but making no headway. The messenger had both feet on the brake lever, fighting to keep the coach from sliding back any further.

Eli came close and shouted, "Your leaders are down! I'm gonna take a look!" and stepped down, dropping the reins of the claybank to ground tie him, and with head ducked, he put one hand on the rump of the right wheel horse, spoke to him as he walked beside him, then to the swing team, and on to the downed leaders. He approached slowly, talking easy, just loud enough to be heard over the storm, and touched the rump of the right leader, moved closer, and saw the horse had a broken leg, bone jutting out of the skin, blood flowing with the rain. He pulled out his Colt, stepped behind the head of the horse, and dropped the hammer to end the horse's suffering. All the horses jerked at the sound of the shot, but Eli stepped past the right leader, to the left. The big black was also down, but one leg was under him, the other stretched out. Eli stroked his neck, talked softly, trying to settle down the panicked horse.

He began to strip the harness from both the downed horses, and once the black was freed, Eli stepped before him and encouraged the big gelding to rise. The animal rocked back on his haunches, rolled side to side, freed his leg and stretched both out before him. Eli was relieved to see both legs were sound, and with more encouragement, he pulled the horse free and away from the others. He tied off the black to a nearby tree, returned to the coach and muscled a couple big rocks behind the front wheels, and looked to the driver, "I think that might hold you, but keep a taut line on your teams, and I'll get the passengers out!" He had to holler to be heard, but the driver acknowledged with a nod.

Standing on the hub of the front wheel, Eli leaned over to the front window and looked to see a full load of very frightened passengers, talking and fussing among themselves. They had the window coverings drawn to keep out the rain, but Eli had pushed one aside, "Alright folks, we're gonna get you out! When you open this door, you'll have to stretch alongside here, step on the spoke of the wheel, then to the ground. I'll be right here to help, but we need to get you out 'fore this thing goes over the edge!"

The door slapped open and a man with a dark suit, black derby, and black eyes tried to push his way until Eli stopped, "Ladies first!" he demanded. The man growled, "Do you know who I am?"

"Don't know, don't care. Now sit back and let the ladies out first!"

"How dare you!" growled the man, pushing his way into the door. Eli gave him a quick backhand, not hard enough to knock him back, but enough to get his attention. He looked at Eli, started grabbing at his inside pocket. Eli snatched the Colt from his own open coat and cocked the hammer as he brought it up while the grump was still grabbing at his coat. When he looked up, the one-eyed man-killing Colt stared at him, and Eli explained, "Ladies first!"

The man dropped back in his seat, nodded to one of the women, and she leaned to the door, grinned at Eli, and reached for his hand. He helped her stretch across to the wheel, held her hand as she dropped to the ground, and directed her, "You might find some shelter in the trees yonder."

Six men and two women came from the coach with Eli's help, and when the coach was emptied, Eli looked at the driver. "Think you can get 'er up now?"

"Dunno, these horses are 'bout wore out trying to keep us from goin' over. But if you go to the head of the swing pair, hold 'em tight while me'n the messenger get down, we can prob'ly get 'em to pull from the front a little better, leastways till we get back on the road!"

Eli walked to the front, stood before the two that were now the leaders of the four-up and with a firm hand on the bridles, he nodded to the jehu and messenger and watched the two men climb down. They walked with stiff legs to the leaders. The driver spoke to Eli, "You're a lifesaver! Thank you kindly." Eli nodded as he reached for the reins of the leader, nodded to the messenger, who did the same, then both men encouraged and tugged at the two, and as the traces drew taut again, the four horses dug into the mud and fought their way free, pulling the coach back onto the roadway.

CHAPTER 22

SUMMIT

The rain continued in a steady drizzle making the muddy road look more like a runoff creek than a roadway for wagons and stagecoaches. The men worked to get the coach on solid ground with the driver up top encouraging the horses and the messenger and Eli by the leaders to pull them aside and back them into the harness. With water dripping off the saggy felt hat, often running down his neck and back, Eli shook his head and struggled with the last of the horses. The messenger was hooking up the other leader and Eli backed the last one into line to hook up to the trace chains. He heard a clatter and rattle of wagons, turned to look down the road to see the big Jutland team in the lead of the first wagon, heads down, hooves sloshing in the mud and the wagon dragging behind. He shook his head, hollered to the messenger, "There come my wagons! We need to get this coach movin'!"

The stage was finally lined out, the single horse tied off at the back. "I reckon we can make it the rest of the way, seein' as how it's all downhill into Ashland! Sure do thank you for helpin' us out!" proclaimed the driver as he climbed back into the driver's box beside the messenger.

"Happy to help!" He nodded down the road, "Those are my wagons coming, try to keep it on the road, but make as much room as you can!" hollered Eli as he stepped back from the coach. He glanced at the windows and one of the women was leaning close and said, "Yes, thank you, sir! It's been a while since we've seen a real gentleman." She smiled and nodded as the coach rocked back on its thoroughbraces and the team leaned into the traces to start the coach down the hill.

Eli sloshed through the mud, sometimes sinking to his boot-tops, the muck and mire sucking at his feet, making Eli think of quicksand. He shook his head, struggling to get to the trees and out of the way of the wagons. He looked down the road just in time to see the first wagon, driven by the broad-shouldered Erik Pedersen, who was leaning into the rain and slapping the horses with the reins, talking all the while to encourage the animals. When Erik saw the coach coming downhill, he stood, pulling hard on the reins to move as far to the uphill side of the road as possible to make room for the coach.

The wagon slipped in the deep gumbo, the horses digging deep with every step sucking at the big hooves, and each lift of a hoof bringing gobs of mud with it, doubling the work of the horses. Eli saw the wagon leaning into the embankment. He caught his breath as it began to topple, and as the coach pushed past, the wagon teetered, but the slap of reins and the shout of Erik caused the big four-up team of Jutland horses to dig even deeper, putting all their massive weight into the effort. With Erik standing on the high side, shifting his weight, and the family pushing up the canvas for them to lean on the high side as well, the big team pulled it back onto the high ground and leveled out.

Eli breathed easy, shaking his head as he watched the big horses, chins tucked to their chests, massive hooves lifting and driving deep, wheels churning through the deep mud like the paddles on a butter churn, and the wagon moved, slowly, almost imperceptibly, but it moved, and they came nearer and nearer. As they came closer, Eli stepped from under the big spruce, pointing up the road, "Keep 'em movin'! Not far to the crest, then it'll be easier!"

Erik nodded, grinning, but keeping his eyes on the team, always shouting encouragement, using the reins to remind them he was there, and he stood, facing into the storm, water dripping from his cap, his nose, his clothes all soaked, the canvas on the wagon drooping between the hoops, but still they churned through the muck and moved.

Behind the Pedersens came the Hansens. With Leif standing much like Erik, but with Olivia on the seat beside him, the youngsters, Asta, Anja, and Harald, in the wagon but with the edges of the canvas lifted so they could see the storm and more. Eli chuckled, shook his head, and watched as the double team responded just like those of the Pedersen wagon, all the horses digging deep, heads down, plodding and pushing through the thick gumbo mud. Eli frowned as he looked, seeing the wheels sinking into the mud halfway to the hub, churning the muck, and making the road more of a mess than before. With one wagon and a stagecoach passing, the water was now standing in the ruts, mixing with the mud with each hoof fall and wheel turn. He watched Leif focusing on the horses, keeping them on the move and slowly making progress. Eli wondered just how bad it would get before the last wagon came.

He heard the deep voice of Marcus Moller, shouting to be heard above the roar of the storm, standing tall in the wagon box, hands full of wet reins, and his four-up of bays looking black in the rain, but the mud was to their knees, each drive of the big hooves digging deeper and deeper, churning the mud into a sucking mire. As Eli watched, the big horses struggled. Suddenly, the nearest leader stumbled, stretched out his neck and fell to his chest, his head in the standing water of the rut just made by the Hansen wagon. Eli lunged from under the tree, rushing to the lead horse, fighting the mud that was almost knee deep, and with each step, the slimy fingers of muck grabbed at his feet. He kept his eyes on the horse that was thrashing, tossing his head to keep out of the water, with the horse beside him also fighting the muck.

Eli stepped beside the big horse whose muzzle was now under water, his eyes closed to keep the rain and mud away, but he snorted, blowing bubbles in the muddy water. Eli dropped to his knees, reached under the jaw of the big horse, and lifted his muzzle from the water, struggling to hold it out of the mud. The big nostrils flared, the eyes flashed open, and the horse knew Eli was helping. As Eli struggled to hold the big head above the water, the horse pawed at the mud, rocking his body side to side to get some footing, and with his big hooves planted deep, he fought to his feet.

Eli was in the mud up to his waist and grabbed for the collar of the big horse, who now gave Eli a tug, and he too rose from the mud, wrapped his arms around the neck of the big horse, and stroked his face, laughing. "Ain't we a pair?!" he chuckled and began fighting his way through the mud to get out of the way of the wagon.

Eli heard Marcus holler, "You alright?"

"Yeah, keep movin'!"

And the slap of reins and the sucking sounds of lifting hooves, accompanied by the creak and groan of the wet wagon, assured Eli the wagon was on the move again. He made his way to the trees but stopped and let the downpour rid him of much of the mud that stuck to every part of the lower half of his body. He walked to where Rusty and Grey stood under the wide-spread branches of a big spruce and dropped to the mat of pine needles, turning around to face the road and watch the progress of the wagons.

He sat with elbows on his knees and hands clasped when Rusty nudged him on the back with his muzzle. Eli laughed, "I know, I know. But remind me again why we're doin' this!" The big stallion nickered as if laughing at Eli, tossed his head, and the Grey joined in, tossing his head as if the two were having a big guffaw at Eli. He sat, shaking his head, wiping water from his face and removed his hat to shake it free of water, then turned his attention to the last wagon.

Anton Lund was on the last wagon, and it had the greatest struggle. With every step of the horses driving deep, the turn of the wheels sloshing, and the box of the wagon rocking side to side, they moved slower, but still they moved, and the big Jutland horses proved their worth. Eli watched as the wagon crept past, and once he saw the back of the wagon, he went to his horses, mounted up, and with the Grey following close behind and Lobo in the lead, they stayed in the trees. By keeping to a small game trail with pine needles for a carpet, they quietly climbed to the crest of the pass.

As the wagons neared the crest, the road split the thick timber, pushed over a wide bending switchback, and surmounted the rocky knob. The roadway was rocky and less muddy but the horses were growing tired yet labored onward. Erik Pedersen sat back in his seat and kept the horses moving but put one foot on the brake lever and held a taut rein on the team.

The road made a wide bend around a shoulder, cut into a long ravine to make a dogleg bend, and took the shelf road around a rocky promontory. As the road straightened, a wide shoulder offered a place to pull off and Erik gladly reined the team onto the wide shoulder and pulled up. He locked the brake lever, grabbed a big brush, stepped down and went to the horses. As he began giving the horses a bit of a rubdown, he lifted his eyes to the sky, relieved the storm had passed, and saw the other wagons also pulling off the road.

As Eli broke from the timber, he saw the back end of Anton's wagon with Candy's horse tied off behind, and Eli grinned, knowing his friend was spending time with Emilie, the sixteen-year-old daughter of the Lund family. Eli shook his head as he chuckled, remembering what it was like to be young and interested in the young ladies, but he also remembered that he never had the opportunity to 'go courting' as most young men. He had spent his time at sea, and upon his return, went to West Point and after graduation was sent west. It was on his first time in the west that Eli's dying friend asked him to take care of his wife, who was expecting. Eli did what was right, married the woman, and became a father to her twins, but the army and the war interfered with his life as a married man and father. He chuckled, thinking he was feeling sorry for himself, and that was not his way. He knew he did what was right, and he did not regret that. But now, that duty still beckoned, and he was determined to fulfill the last promise to his wife and find the twins. "If we ever get outta these mountains and get shed of these wagons!" he muttered to himself.

Chapter 23

California

"Been havin' any trouble up this way? You know, with natives, outlaws, that sort?" asked Eli. He was sitting at the table inside the Cottonwood Relay station for the California Stagecoach Company visiting with Homer Updike, the station operator. As was his habit and whenever he had the opportunity, Eli would glean all the information about the trail, the people, and more from anyone that knew the area—and he knew there was no one better nor more talkative than a stage station keeper.

"Oh, not so's you'd notice. All the '49'rs an' others, you know, vigilantes, soldiers, purty well took care th' Injuns. Those that weren't massacreed, they rounded up an' put on reservations. Course there has been some talk that there's some o' them Modocs from over to Tule lake are tryin' to bust out o' Fort Klamath, but they cain't do it, but if they was to, they could cause lots o' problems, yesirree." He cackled as he sipped the last of his coffee, which was hot enough and thick enough to polish his boots.

Eli chuckled at his response, glanced to Candy, who was leaning back in his chair, balancing it on the back legs as he looked out the one window. Candy grinned, dropped the chair down, and leaned on the table. He looked at the station keeper, "What about the outlaws? Before I left from the rancho, there had been talk of several outlaw gangs that have been havin' their way with wagons and such."

"Where's your rancho?" asked Homer, frowning at Candy, wondering about him because he was dressed in his Charro attire and looked every bit the native Mexican.

Candy grinned, "It's the Rancho Monte del Diablo, Señor Juan Salvio Pacheco. It is east of San Francisco."

"Well then, you might know that most of the outlaw gangs, like those of Tiburcio Vásquez or Procopio Busta-mante and others, have done most of their raiding down south. Although there's been talk of some of their men coming north, I've heard of a Narciso Bojorques that was working east of Eureka, but those are just rumors."

Eli dropped his eyes to his coffee. His cup was only half full, but the brew was too black to see the bottom. He lifted the bitter brew and took a swallow, almost choked and set the cup down. He looked at Homer, who was chuckling, and Eli said, "We prob'ly won't have to worry about natives or outlaws if we drink any more of this rattlesnake venom!"

―――

BRILLIANT GOLD HUNG on the bottoms of the thin line of clouds, the early morning glow giving a golden cast to the hills as the darkness snuffed out the last of its lanterns and was chased away by the morning's light as the wagons stretched out on the trail. They had spent a day and a half camped beside the relay station, resting and cleaning their gear. Now, with the warmth of the morning sun, they were excited about moving south into California. The road sided Cottonwood Creek until the confluence with the Klamath River. Five miles alongside the Klamath brought them to the confluence with the Shasta River that took a round-about course in the shadow of the Klamath Mountains and the Cascade Range before bringing them to Yreka.

They were three days out of Oregon, and with little to offer other than a site to rest the animals, they chose to take a half-day and check over their equipment. Eli and Candy looked over the settlement that had sprung from the gold rush of '51 and Thompson's Dry Diggings in Rocky Gulch. One café with a faded sign, sun-bleached lapboard siding, and a rickety boardwalk in front was the sole offering for a place to eat. The two men looked at one another, laughed, shrugged, and stepped into the shady interior. Four tables, all empty, and a short counter with four stools and an old-timer of sorts leaning against it was the extent of interior decorations, but the old-timer grinned a two-tooth smile and waved them over to the counter. "So, what'll it be, fellas?"

"What's on the menu?" asked Eli as he straddled a stool and leaned on the counter.

"Menu? Hah! We ain't never had one o' them! It's stew or stew. 'Course if'n you want breakfast, we have some left-over stew and a couple flapjacks."

"We'll try your stew," chuckled Eli, glancing to a grinning Candy.

The old man turned away, went to the stove in the corner, grabbed a couple tin plates, scooped up some stew with a big ladle, picked up a handful of biscuits, and plopped it all down in front of the two. He walked back to the stove, and with a couple tin cups and the coffee pot, he returned to the counter, poured the cups full of something black and steaming, and leaned back to look at his customers. "Anythin' else?"

Eli answered, "Maybe some information," and glanced at Candy. Eli dropped his eyes, said a quick, silent prayer of thanks, and started in on the stew. He frowned, looked at the cook, took another bite, and said, "This is good!"

"Wal, of course! How'dya think I stayed in bizness all this time?" he huffed and shook his head as if insulted as he crossed his arms over his chest.

"So, Yreka is a bit unusual of a name, Indian?" asked Candy.

The old man coughed, spat at the spittoon in the corner, shook his head, "Nope. I'll tell you what Bret Harte said 'bout that. He was comin' through here, saw a sign that was freshly painted on some canvas and the letters bled through. He saw it from the back side, and the sign said Bakery. But the b did not bleed through, and some stranger saw it, read it as *yreka*, and thought that was the name of the camp. So, it stuck!"

Eli thought about it, frowned, nodded his under-standing, and chuckled. He looked at the cook, "Been here long?"

"Since '51!"

"We're travelin' with some wagons and are going south on the Oregon-California trail, what some call the Siskiyou. Have you heard anything about it, you know, trouble with natives or others?"

"Ain't been no trouble with the natives, but I been hearin' 'bout some o' them Mexicans," he started, glanced at Candy, and back at Eli, "them what's outlaws.

Since Vásquez and García were part o' that feud down in Monterey seems like ever' two-bit wannabe tries to outdo 'em. But there ain't been much o' that this far north. But the further south you go, best keep yore eyes open!"

———

AFTER TWO LONG days of traversing the long scablands with nothing but bunch grass, basaltic rock, greasewood, and chaparral, the rolling hills had grown monotonous. But the distant Mount Shasta stood like a beacon in the south with crevices filled with glaciers and granite slopes towering above the hills. They pushed on as the timbered foothills of the Klamath mountains shouldered closer to west edge of the Shasta River basin, and the Cascade Range, anchored by Mount Shasta, pushed closer from the east. Even the air was cooler.

Eli, well out front and scouting for the wagons, crossed the narrow creek where it met the Shasta River and neared the timber and the mountains. After crossing the low rise between the buttes, the road followed a smaller creek known as Boles Creek, one of the little run-off creeks fed by the snow melt from Mount Shasta. With a long look at the distant towering peak, he stood in his stirrups and took in a deep breath of the pine-scented mountain air.

"That's him, that's the scout!" declared Juan Soto, the sharpshooter for the newly gathered gang of Narciso Bojorques. Narciso looked at his second, Procopio Busta-mante, who nodded his agreement, and Narciso told Juan, "*Sacarlo!*"

Juan grinned and turned back toward the trail. Although they were on a timber-covered knoll, the clearing offered a break in the trees that gave a clear line of sight to the roadway below. Juan was stretched out belly down on a big rock. He lifted the big Sharps with a telescopic sight and narrowed his aim. His target had stopped and now stood in his stirrups as if daring Juan to take his shot. Juan grinned, took a breath, let some out, and slowly squeezed the trigger. The big rifle bucked and roared, spat smoke, fire, and lead, the blast rumbling through the big trees. The horses of the men behind him jerked and stepped back, but were settled by their riders.

Eli heard the report of the big buffalo gun and felt the impact to the side of his head. He grabbed at his head as he slid from the saddle. He frowned, confused at the blackness, but did not feel the ground when he crashed down into the manzanita at the side of the road. Rusty spooked away into the timber, the grey on his heels. Lobo had been out front, and when the big stallion clattered into the trees, the wolf whimpered and followed. Silence settled on the timber, no birds sang, no chipmunks scolded, and even the far away creek seemed to have silenced. The figure on the ground lay unmoving as the dust settled around the edge of the roadway and the brush that hid the prone body.

CHAPTER 24

MOONLIGHT

The Flying Cloud lay at anchor in San Francisco Bay. With the load of lumber off-loaded and the agent bartering and bickering for additional cargo. The clipper had all sails furled, and the moonlight danced across the ripples of the bay as the quiet evening invited all ages to enjoy the beautiful night. Standing at the rail on the forecastle were two couples, apart from one another, but sharing the moment and the mood. They were a familiar sight to all aboard, although they thought their rendezvous was in secret, but they had been meeting at every opportunity afforded. Whenever the watch of the two brothers allowed, they met with the girls that now leaned against the railing, pulling the young men close with their shy smiles and whispered thoughts.

Jubal's hands sat at the waist of Gabrielle while her hands rested on his shoulders. "I was happy to find out you were not going ashore. What happened?" he asked, holding her close.

"Oh, Mother decided she did not want to visit her

sister after all and wanted to go home. Of course, we didn't argue with her because that gave us more time with you!" She smiled coyly at the young man, "I just couldn't bear the thought of leaving you," she pouted and added, "I never thought love could be like this," she sighed, smiling. "I've read so many books, like Pride and Prejudice, Great Expectations, and swooned as I read them, but I never imagined what it would be like to experience those feelings."

"I never thought much about love, until I saw you," replied Jubal. "It's hard to believe it's only been just over a month since we first talked, and now I'm thinkin' I've known you all my life."

Gabrielle smiled, "Me too, but what do we do now? Our home in Monterey is only a few days away, and Mother is already making plans for another trip. After being together almost every night, if just for a few moments, I can't stand the thought of being away from you!" she pleaded, leaning her cheek against his chest.

"I dunno. Josh and I have been talking—" he began, but Gabrielle looked up at him and interrupted, "So have we," nodding to her sister, Gisèle, who leaned into Joshua's arms a few feet away and also beside the rail.

Jubal chuckled, "And what have you two been thinking?"

Gabrielle smiled and leaned to the side to motion to her sister and Joshua to come near. Gisèle grabbed Joshua's hand and led him to the side of the others, smiling and giggling, "What?"

Gabrielle smiled at her sister, looked back to Jubal, and said, "We think you should come home with us!"

"Come home with you?! And then what?" asked Jubal, looking to his brother, who showed a wide-eyed and surprised expression on his otherwise stoic face.

"Why, get married, silly!" she declared, leaning against Jubal's chest and smiling up at him.

Jubal matched Joshua's expression with one of his own that was just as flabbergasted, "Married?! We can't get married! We are on a ship and don't know where we're going and when and...and...we could get into all kinds of trouble!" he grumbled, looking to Joshua for help.

Josh chuckled, "We *were* shanghaied, and we didn't sign any contract. I checked with Whitcomb; he said the Merchant's Seamen Act only applies if we signed a contract. If we jump ship, even if they caught us, there's nothing they can do except return us to the ship, and even that wouldn't be lawful."

"So, you've been thinkin' about this too?" asked Jubal, glancing from one to the other of the conspirators. He shook his head, looked at Gabrielle, and asked, "What about your mother? Won't she be just a little upset?"

The girls looked at one another, laughing, "Mother! She's been wanting to get us married off since we were fourteen! Sometimes I think she'd be glad to get shed of us so she can do all the traveling she wants without having to worry about us!" grumbled Gabrielle. She turned a smiling face to Jubal, scooted closer, slipped her hand through his arm, and pulled close, "Don't you want to be with us?"

Jubal let a slow grin split his face, shook his head as he looked to his brother, glanced around the forecastle and saw the first watch busy with their duties, which were minimal when lying at anchor. He sighed heavily, looked at the others, and began, "Alright, what have you been thinking?"

––––––

SIX BELLS on the morning watch saw Jubal and Joshua as crew of the gig under the direction of the coxswain, Whitcomb, and the other two crew were Riley and James, the same crew as before when they were tasked with shuttling the agent and some passengers to and from the ship. The gig was alongside as the agent climbed down and dropped into his customary seat. He was a rather surly fellow, and none of the crew liked him, nor did he like anyone aboard ship, the captain included. But his need of going ashore offered the opportunity the twins were seeking.

Since the *Flying Cloud* had offloaded her cargo, she had to yield the wharf to other ships until additional cargo had been contracted for and would need to be loaded. In the meantime, there was shore leave for some of the men, but the captain was wary of letting those that had been shanghaied have the same freedom.

The *Flying Cloud* was anchored in deep water in the bay and well south of the Isla de Yerba Buena. A direct line from the ship to the wharf was just less than four miles, but the water was calm and the day bright, with just a slight breeze to cool the men hard at work on the oars. Jubal and Joshua looked at the other ships, some at the wharves, some at anchor, and noticed both sailing ships and steamships. Another clipper, the *White Swallow,* was anchored just north of the *Cloud.* They pushed past the barque *Speedwell* and the schooner *Fanny Gilmor.* The British ship *Moneta* was at a wharf near the barque *R.W. Wood.* When the agent saw the schooner *James M. Waterbury,* he huffed and shook his head, mumbling, "Never seen the like! That schooner has a colored man for their captain! Captain George Brooks, and the Notary that made up the shipping articles and affidavits was also a colored man!" he shook his head and grumbled some more, but the attention of the men turned to the ships.

They passed a steamer, the *Golden Age,* rated at 2200 tons, that was docked at the Pacific Mail Steamship Company wharf. Opposite the *Golden Age* was the *Moses Taylor,* another Pacific steamship that was known to carry over seven hundred passengers and considerable cargo as well. Jubal glanced to Joshua, and both were thinking about the crews of these ships and wondering if any were thinking about jumping ship, for the San Francisco Bay offered several towns and many places to hide or even find work, whether on another ship or somewhere on dry land.

The agent directed the coxswain to go to the docks at the end of Market Street, "And you men stay by the boat! I might be most of the day, but if I get enough cargo earlier, I'll be wanting to get back to the ship to tell the captain."

"Yessir, whatever you say, sir!" answered Whitcomb, showing his most stoic face with a deeply furrowed brow. He leaned into the tiller to steer the gig alongside an empty wharf and into the sandy beach. With a nod to the two oarsmen at the forward spot, they lifted their oars, jumped into the water, and hauled the boat further ashore, allowing the agent to step onto dry sand.

After the agent walked away, satchel under his arm and derby cocked at a jaunty angle, the men watched, and the coxswain Whitcomb mimicked the man with his cocky strut that did little to compliment the agent. Jubal glanced to Joshua, nodded, and turned to Whitcomb, "How's about lettin' us go ashore, maybe get us somethin' to eat an' look around a mite?"

Whitcomb had overheard some of the whispered

plans of the twins and stepped closer to Jubal, lowered his voice, and answered, "I'll delay as long as I can. But like I told your brother, the Merchant Seaman's Act only applies if you signed a contract. But that doesn't mean the captain didn't make up a phony contract with your names on it and use that to send the constables after you. So, if you do this, you hightail it outta town and make yourselves scarce. Don't leave any sign behind, and don't stay in town!"

"Thanks, Whit, you're alright," replied Jubal, nodding to his brother. He slapped Whitcomb on the shoulder and spoke louder for the others to hear, "I'll get us all somethin' to eat! No tellin' when that agent will get back. I'm guessin' he won't return till dark!" He shook his head, motioned for Joshua to follow, and they started up the shore, stomped onto the cobblestone of Market Street, and with a wave back to the men on the gig, turned away and disappeared.

CHAPTER 25

BANDITOS

Anton Lund sat beside his wife, Freja, and slapped reins to the four-up team of Jutland horses, pushing them to cross at the confluence of the creek and the Shasta River that soon sided the rocky and timber-covered foothills of the Cascades. As the leaders started through the shallow stream, Anton looked at his wife, "This is where Eli said the road cuts back into the hills." He paused and lifted his eyes to the distant Mount Shasta that stood like a lone sentinel, its granite peak appearing to scratch at the blue of the sky as it clutched icy glaciers in the narrow ravines. "Look at that. You don't see mountains like that very often!"

Freja elbowed her husband in the ribs, "Anton!" she muttered.

He glanced to her, saw she was frowning and not looking at the mountain but nodding toward them on the far side of the river. He slapped reins to the team, pushing them across the water, watching the two men that sat on their horses in the road, waiting. His first thought was they were waiting until the wagons crossed, so he gave them no mind, but their expression was anything but friendly or even curious. The men were obviously Mexican, both wearing big sombreros and riding the typical Mexican saddle with the tapaderos and big pommel. Behind them, the road started a short climb to cross over a saddle between two low buttes, but the men did not move, forcing Anton to rein up the big team.

"Excuse me, but we need to get by, there are three other wagons coming," said Anton, standing and looking at the two men.

The two men nodded, grinning, looked to one another, and said something in Spanish but were not loud enough nor clear enough for Anton to understand, although he did understand some Spanish. They laughed, and the obvious leader looked at Anton as he pushed the sombrero off his head to hang at his back. "Si, si, señor, I unnerstan', you want us to move so you can bring our wagons across the reever, si, si." He chuckled but did not move, he pointed to the side of the road beside Anton's wagon and said, "There ees room," pointing to the wide shoulder of the road, "an' there ees more room behin' you," pointing behind him at the wagon of Leif Hansen that was crossing the river. "We weel wait for theem."

"What do you mean?"

The speaker lifted a pistol and motioned to Anton, "Thees is what I mean! We weel wait for theem," motioning for Anton to be seated.

"Now, hold on! You can't order us around! We will not wait!" He slapped reins to the horses and hollered, "Giddup horses!" The big team leaned into their collars, trace chains rattled, and as the big team dropped their heads and dug with their hooves, the pistol barked, and the leader horse dropped in his harness as if poleaxed. The bullet shattered its way through the thick skull of the big horse and killed it instantly. The other horses spooked, sidestepping, the racketing echo of the pistol shot, and the smell of blood startled them, but Anton pulled a taut rein, "Whoa boys, whoa…" his eyes flared, his temper rose, and he shouted, "You! You! There was no reason to do that! You killed him!"

"Si, si, an' I weel keel you too!" The man lifted his pistol, and it barked again. The bullet took Anton in his upper chest, to be followed almost instantly by another that shattered his solar plexus, and the big man fell over the footrest of the driver's box to tumble to the ground. Freja screamed, stood with wide eyes, and reached out to Anton, but he was unmoving, eyes staring into nothing. She put her hand to her mouth and sat down, staring at the two men, fear painting her face as she trembled in the seat. With her hand to her mouth, she spoke softly, turning her head slightly to be heard by her children in the wagon, "Emilie, take the children and run into the trees, don't let them see you! Hurry!" She heard the rustle of movement and watched the two men as they looked at the other wagons.

————

LEIF HANSEN WAS DRIVING the second wagon and had heard what he thought was gunfire, and with the Lund wagon stopped, he reined his team to the side of the road to pull beside the Lund wagon, but the children were jumping out, and the team almost trampled the boy, Olaf. Lief frowned, "Here, here! What're you doin'?" he spoke to Emilie, but she shushed him with a motion to her mouth, and as the wagon pulled beside theirs, she herded the two children before her, and they dropped off the road into the cottonwoods and manzanita.

Lief saw the body of Anton as he reined up his team, looked at Freja, and said, "What—" but his attention was immediately taken by the two gunmen. He slammed his foot against the brake lever to lock it in place and leaned down to get his rifle, but a bullet took him in the neck, and he crumpled into the bottom of the driver's box to the scream of his wife, Olivia.

The one man that had done all the talking looked at his partner, who held a smoking pistol before him, "Why deed you do that?" he asked, shaking his head.

The man shrugged, grinned, and motioned with his chin to the third wagon that came from the river to pull behind the Lund wagon. "I weel go to that one!" declared Procopio Bustamante, grinning and holding his pistol before him. "You take care of theese wimmen, I weel bring the others!"

The Pedersen wagon, driven by Erik, pulled up behind the Lund wagon and stopped as Erik set his brake. At the same time, Bustamante trotted his horse close. He was grinning as he waved his pistol, "You weel get down, señor. Now!"

"What? What's this all about?" asked Erik, frowning at the man as he wrapped the reins around the brake lever.

"Just come weeth me, señor, and you too, señora!" He motioned with his pistol, "Do you wan' to die too?" he threatened, waving the pistol and grinning broadly, showing tobacco-stained teeth, with two missing at the side of his mouth.

As Erik helped his wife, Alma, she muttered, "The children?" but was commanded by the outlaw, "No talking!"

They were herded forward by Bustamante to stand beside the Lund wagon. Alma looked up at Freja, who was sobbing into her handkerchief, her shoulders shaking. She did not hear when Alma asked, "Are you alright?"

The leader, Narciso Bojorques, ordered Bustamante, "Obtener los otros!" and waved his pistol at his second, who reined his horse around and started to the back of the wagons. Erik Pedersen demanded, "What do you want? Why are you doing this?"

Narciso leaned on his pommel, his pistol pointed at Erik, and answered, "We wan' your gold an' your valuables, all of them!" he chuckled as he looked from Alma to Freja.

As Bustamante rode to the back of the wagons, three other banditos splashed across the river, the leader Juan Soto, shaking his head. He looked at Bustamante, "The other one, the vaquero, ees not here." He shrugged and reined up beside Procopio. The last wagon had pulled up beside that of the Pedersens, and the two men rode to the far side. They came up from behind the wagon and startled Marcus when Bustamante said, "Get down! Now!" as he waved his pistol threateningly.

Marcus, the big man that he was, frowned at the outlaw, "Who are you?! What are you doing?!" he demanded.

Bustamante said, "We are going to make your wagons lighter. We want all your gold!" he cackled. Marcus reached to wrap the reins around the brake lever, but the outlaw thought he was reaching for a weapon and shot. The bullet bore through the big man's shoulder, making him drop the reins and spook the horses, but the brake held, and Marcus grunted, "Easy boys, easy."

Ida Moller had stifled her scream but reached to her

husband to pull him back in the seat. She glared at the outlaws, "He was just tying off the reins!" she snarled through gritted teeth. Her nostrils flared as she tried to help her man, who was struggling to get down from the wagon. Her hand came back bloody, but she wiped it on the canvas and followed her husband to the ground. She spoke softly to the children, "Stay in the wagon, be quiet!" She coughed, pretending to clear her throat to cover what was said, and followed her wounded husband to the front of the other wagons.

As they stood near the front of the wagons, the two men, Marcus Moller and Erik Pedersen, and their wives, Ida and Alma, were beside the Lund wagon. Freja had forced herself to control her sobbing but still sat in the driver's box. Olivia Hansen had been ordered to take her place beside the others. Bojorques glared at each one, focused on Erik, and demanded, "Where ees your gold?!"

"Gold? What gold? We have no gold!" pleaded Erik, looking at the outlaw and glancing at the women and Marcus.

"I know you have gold! Eef you do not get it, we weel have to go through your wagons and find it! That will make me ver' angry! When I get angry, I have to keel something!" He glared and snarled at Erik, then waved his pistol at him and the women.

Marcus looked at Erik, "Give it to them, Erik. It will be no good to us if we're dead!" The women chimed in, "Yes, give it to them!" they pleaded.

Narciso Bojorques grinned, "Si, geev eet to us!" he cackled, "or I weel shoot one of your wimmen!" waving the pistol from one to the other.

"Alright, alright!" declared Erik, lifting his hand in surrender. "It's in my wagon!" he explained as he turned to go to his wagon.

Bojorques motioned for Juan Soto to go with him, and the sharpshooter nudged his horse to closely follow Erik to his wagon. Juan watched Erik, and as he neared the wagon, Juan said, "Stop!" He stepped down from his horse, pistol in hand and went to the wagon. He pushed aside the canvas, saw movement in the darkness of the wagon, hollered, "Get out!" and stepped back. The two boys, Niels, sixteen, and Lucas, fourteen, climbed over the tailgate and stepped down. The girl, Nanna, ten, stood at the tailgate as Niels fumbled with the chain to lower the gate. As he did, he lifted his arms and helped his sister to the ground. Juan looked into the wagon, turned, and motioned for Erik to get the gold.

Erik dug around in the wagon as Juan watched, finally uncovered a metal lockbox, retrieved it, turned back, and sat it on the tailgate. Movement caught his eye and he looked up, but the motion was seen by Juan, who turned to see Candy sitting on his mount with a pistol in his hand. Both pistols barked and spat smoke and lead, the bullet from Juan's taking Candy in the lower side, knocking him from his horse. As he slid to the ground, he hollered to his mount, "Go, boy! Go!" Candy's bullet had taken Juan in the throat and he crumpled to the ground, but not before the other two men who had ridden with him came on the run to the wagon just in time to see their friend fall to his face. Clodoveo Chavez looked from his friend to Erik, "Where ees the gold?" he demanded, and Erik pointed to the lockbox. Chavez grabbed the box, glanced at the unmoving body of Candy, and waved his pistol toward Erik to motion him and the children back to the others.

When Narciso saw the box, he stepped down, grabbed the box, and looked at Erik, demanding, "Open eet!"

Erik produced a key, unlocked the box and stepped back. Narciso opened the lid, grinned when he saw several gold coins, some currency, and other coins. He lifted a leather pouch, opened it, and grinned as he reached in to draw out a small handful of gold dust. He laughed, looked at Marcus and Erik, and said, "Seee, you did have some gold! Now I have some gold. But I want more!" He stood, frowning and snarling, waving his pistol at the two men, "Where ees the rest of the gold?!"

"That's all, there is no more!" pleaded Erik, holding his open palms out before him as he pleaded.

"I do not believe you! I theenk I will keel someone!" he cackled, looking at the four women, two men, and the three youngsters that now stood beside their mother. "Wheech one shall I keel?" he asked as he walked toward the children. "Maybe I keel the leetle girl!" he laughed. Alma grabbed her daughter close and declared, "No! There is no more gold!" she explained, hugging her daughter closer.

"Maybe so, we weel see. But if my men find any more gold, we weel keel them all!" he growled as he waved his pistol toward them. He nodded to the men, "Search the wagons!"

CHAPTER 26

SURVIVORS

The rough, wet tongue brought his eyes open, but he learned long ago to never move until he knew his surroundings. The hot breath of Lobo as he lay belly down beside him brought Eli to consciousness. He looked about, felt the crushing weight of pain bearing down on the side of his head, and instinctively slowly moved his hand to the side of his head. It came away with wet and dried blood. He frowned, looking at Lobo and casting his eyes about the brush where he lay. The red bark and brilliant green leaves told him he was in a tangle of manzanita. As he lay still, he heard the sound of rushing water and the ripple of leaves in a breeze, as well as the chatter of a chipmunk, the trill and chirp of the colorful tanager that sat on a tree branch nearby, and the rattle of a woodpecker digging for his morning meal.

Nothing told of alarm or danger, so Eli slowly sat up, the movement aggravating the pain in his head. He put his hand in his hair, felt blood and a groove that cut through his scalp that he recognized as the graze of a bullet. He breathed heavily, looking about, spotted his hat, and reached for it. His head throbbed, making him squint and stifle a groan. He looked at Lobo, "Where's the horses, boy?" he asked, running his hand through the scruff of the wolf's neck. Eli frowned as he looked at the light, recognized the early morning brilliance of the rising sun off his right shoulder, and frowned, *have I been here all night?* He stretched out his legs, moved his arms, rolled his shoulders, and nodded to himself to answer the question, *Guess so.*

A large rock was beside him, the manzanita all about, and he slowly stood to look around. Lobo had padded off, and Eli looked about. *I was riding there,* he thought as he looked at the road and the spruce and pine that crowded the base of the hill on the far side. *I heard a shot just as I was hit. Whoever did it must have thought I was dead or were too lazy to look through the brush. Where's the wagons?* When he realized he was alone, his stomach twisted in knots, knowing that something was wrong. If no one had come looking for him, it must have been because they were not able, and that would mean trouble.

He started pushing his way through the tangle, snagged his trousers on some thorny wild rose bushes, but forced his way into the clear. He made a quick check of his weapons and had the Colt under thong in the holster, the LeMat still in his belt at his back, and the Bowie knife in its scabbard at his side. He stood beside the road, looking about as he stretched and arched his back. He heard movement in the trees and ducked back to the bushes, but saw Lobo bolt from the tree line, tongue lolling and his long legs bounding, followed closely by Rusty and Grey. Eli grinned and walked to meet the horses, stroking the head of each one, talking to them. He saw a break in the brush, led the horses to water, stripped the saddles and gear, and rubbed them both down with a handful of dry grass.

As they grazed, Eli washed his wound as best he could, grabbed a handful of fresh, green leaves from the manzanita, and began chewing them into a poultice. He swallowed much of the juice, knowing it was good for headaches, and he could use some relief. He plastered the poultice on the side of his head, covering the long wound as best he could and used his hat to hold it in place. He fetched some jerky from the saddle bags, picked a couple handfuls of bright red manzanita berries, used a cup to get some fresh water, and made a quick breakfast, sharing some with Lobo, who lay belly down, grinning at the antics of Eli. He cut some strips from the edge of his blanket, chewed some more manzanita, and changed the poultice, determined to replace the tight-fitting hat with a bandage that would do a better job of holding the poultice in place and not put so much pressure on the wound.

He sat beside Lobo, looked at the horses, and thought about the wagons. "Well boys, I reckon we need to go lookin' for some wagons," he drawled as he stood, stretched and began saddling the horses. He had already looked at the road nearby and there were no fresh wagon tracks, so they could not have come this far. *Now, they're either camped back by the river or..."* He shook his head, winced at the pain, stepped into the stirrup, swung a leg over the cantle, and settled into the saddle. He waved for Lobo to take the lead, looked to see if Grey was following, and nudged the big stallion to the road. As they stepped onto the roadway, Eli loosened the Winchester in the scabbard, removed the thong from the Colt, and prepared himself for whatever was to come.

A stagecoach sat in the middle of the road, the four

wagons close together between the road and the river. Eli reined up next to the tree line, unseen by those near the wagons. Something was wrong. The teams had been unhitched and grazed near the river, a crude corral had been fashioned with brush and ropes, one man stood beside the stage talking to the driver. A few youngsters were sitting together on the river bank, but none were playing, and no others showed.

As Eli nudged Rusty forward, the driver of the stage cracked his whip over the heads of the six-up and the stage started across the shallow river, the lone man from the wagons standing, hands on hips, watching the stage leave. He turned back to the wagons, caught a glimpse of the rider coming, stepped close to the wagons, and snatched up a rifle. Eli frowned, doffed his hat, waved it to the wagons, nudged Rusty to a trot, and rode up to the camp. Erik lifted the rifle, recognized Eli, and called out, "Eli!" He turned to the wagons, "Eli's back!"

As he neared, Eli frowned as he glanced about. Two fresh graves were under the trees at the edge of the grass, crude crosses standing at the head. He expected to see all the families, youngsters included, but only Erik stood, although he saw movement coming from one of the wagons where a woman was climbing down from the back. "What happened?" asked Eli as he stepped down from the saddle. "Whose graves?"

Erik lowered the rifle and dropped his eyes, "Mexican banditos! They hit us just after we crossed, killed Anton and Leif." He pointed to the graves, "Shot Marcus too, but he's gonna be alright."

"Candy?" asked Eli, looking expectantly at the lone man.

"He's in a wagon yonder. Freja and Olivia are tendin' him. He was shot too. They thought he was dead, that's the only reason he's still alive. And… and…" he shook his head, grinding his teeth in anger, hit his leg with a fist, "they took Asta and Anja, Leif's girls."

"Anything else?" asked Eli, looking around at the wagons and the circle of young'uns.

"They got most of our ready cash, but that don't mean nothin' after what they done."

Eli frowned and looked at Erik, "Whaddya mean, 'most' of your cash?"

"We still have the biggest part, the gold, hidden in a false bottom of two wagons. They didn't know about that, but that's not important now." He shook his head and looked at Eli, "What are we gonna do now?" he pleaded. "I'm the only man left! I can't leave all these women and kids! And even if I found 'em, then what?" He kicked at a pebble, the muscles in his face flexing as he slowly shook his head, "I know, I know, if it was my girl, I'd go anyway, but…"

"How many were there?" asked Eli.

"There were five, but Candy killed one." He looked up at Eli, "They came at us when we didn't expect it! Before we were across the river, they shot Anton, killed him, and when Leif pulled up beside him, they shot him too! The rest of us didn't see them until after we crossed. We didn't know why the other wagons stopped until we were confronted by their guns. Leif tried for his rifle, and they shot him down! Never said a word, just killed him! And then they threatened to kill the women and children!" He was almost shouting when he told of the happening, his anger and frustration showing as he gestured and stomped around.

Eli lifted one hand, open palm held out, "Easy, Erik, easy. The women and children need you to be strong now, just settle down." He paused and glanced around, "Which wagon is Candy in?"

Erik pointed to the second wagon beside the road, "My wagon, there."

Eli dropped the reins of Rusty to ground-tie him and started to the wagon. Erik stood staring at his back, watching him walk to the wagons. As he neared, Eli called out to those in the wagon, "It's Eli, alright if I come in?"

"Yes, Eli, come on in," answered Freja.

The canvas had been pushed aside and Eli stepped up on the tailgate, ducked under the hoops and stepped into the wagon. He had doffed his hat and caught the reaction of Freja as she saw the makeshift bandage and frowned.

"What happened to you?" she asked, standing and looking at his bandage.

"Same bunch musta shot me outta the saddle 'fore they hit you. Just woke up this mornin'."

"Let me take a look at that!" declared Freja. "You sit down right there!" she demanded, motioning to the big box that sat to the side of the wagon box, opposite the bed where Candy lay.

Eli chuckled, looked at Candy, saw he was awake, attentive, and grinning. "You just can't help yourself, can you. Anytime you can get a woman to fuss over you, you'll do whatever it takes to get some attention!"

"Si, amigo. But it is nothing. Just enough to get the ladies to look at my muscles!" he chuckled but winced at the pain.

Eli frowned as Freja pulled off his bandage, touched the poultice, and made a face. "What is this?" she asked, picking at the poultice to remove it.

"That's manzanita leaves, a good native remedy. And

chewing the leaves helps with my headache!" he protested as she continued to remove the poultice.

She clucked her tongue as she shook her head, "Men! You're all alike, think you know everything!"

Eli tried to ignore Freja as she did her best to tend to his wound. He looked at Candy and asked, "Bad?"

"Not so bad. Are you going?" Candy motioned with his hand to indicate a pursuit of the outlaws.

"Yeah. I'll see if I can pick up their trail, and…" he shrugged, knowing the task he considered would be difficult at best, if not impossible. One man against four desperate outlaws and them having a day's head start. He shook his head at the thought and winced when Freja grabbed his chin to make him hold still.

Candy said, "Give me time to get ready, I'll come with you!"

"You'll do no such thing! You're in no condition to ride. You'll bust that wound open and start bleeding again, and no tellin' what will happen then!" scolded Olivia, shaking her finger at Candy.

CHAPTER 27

TRAIL

Erik's two boys, Neils and Lucas, had rounded up Candy's buckskin, Sundowner, and at Erik's word, they saddled him, and he stood ready, waiting for Candy. They watched as Candy tenderly stepped from the wagon, holding his side where the women had bound his midriff tightly, and kept a tight grip on the edge of the wagon box as he stepped to the ground, wincing at the movement and the impact. He shook his head, lifted his eyebrows and with renewed determination. His teeth clenched, he stretched out to grab the big saddle horn, lifted his foot into the stirrup, took a deep breath and rose to stand. He gently swung his leg over the cantle and dropped into the saddle. He sat straight, stiff, and unmoving as he settled into the seat, resolved to make the ride to find the girls and the outlaws.

Candy looked at Eli, forced a bit of a grin, and nodded slightly. Eli nodded, stepped aboard his claybank stallion, glanced at Erik and the women, looked for Lobo and Grey, and started back to the river.

Their initial search showed the tracks of five horses going back to the river crossing. Erik had said the men caught the horse of the dead man and used it to carry the two girls. They splashed across the river, spotted the tracks that turned upriver and started off.

Where the main road or trail turned away from the Shasta River to cross over closer to Mount Shasta, the river came from the lesser mountain to the west. It was wild country, timber was sparse, intermingled with grassy parks and flats, but the higher it climbed up the shoulders of the mountain, the thicker the timber, but the trail of the outlaws continued without stopping.

Eli reined up at the edge of a small meadow, looking across the grassy flat and letting his eyes rove to the southwest and up the shoulders of the big mountain. Several long ridges stretched into the valley from higher up. Long, deep ravines divided the finger-like ridges, each carrying water to add to the Shasta. But the biggest of the ridges was topped by a bald granite tipped peak that stood head and shoulders above the rest, with the upper reaches showing dusky gold and grey granite that stood above timberline. Eli looked at Candy, "They're moving without hurrying and without stopping. They believe no one will be following."

Candy chuckled, "Si, si. They think we are both dead!" He paused, his lip starting to curl, and with anger, he added, "And they killed two of the other men, wounded the third, and left the smallest one to take care of the women and kids. They know one man would not come after them. They saw all the men with *desprecio*, thought they were cowards. That's why they shot them!"

"You're right, they think we're dead and they have no worries about anyone following. But they're still moving without stopping—that tells me they have a camp or hideout up on that mountain somewhere and they're wanting to get there. If it was far, they would stop to rest the horses—this is a long climb, but not if they're getting close."

He looked at the sun, saw it nearing its zenith, then stood in his stirrups and stretched to look up the mountain. There was no sign of smoke, no movement or sound, but he was certain he was right. "Maybe they have a cabin up there. You know, some old prospector cabin or something."

"What should we do now?" asked Candy.

Eli was quiet for a moment, looking toward the big mountain but searching the flats before it. He frowned, sat back in the saddle, withdrew his binoculars, grinned, lowered the field glasses and looked to Candy, "There's a farm yonder. Looks like it's been here a while. Let's ride over there and talk to 'em, they might be some help."

———

A WELL-BUILT log home with a steep roof that showed a high-up window—which told of a loft room—and several windows on the main floor, with a stone chimney with a wisp of smoke rising above, told of a family that took pride in what they had and built things to last. The big barn had double doors, shuttered windows, and a hay loft. Corrals were connected to the barn, accessible from the rear doors, and smaller buildings probably stored tack and other equipment.

Several head of cattle grazed in a green meadow beyond the barn, and horses trotted to the fence to look at the visitors. A storm cellar had a chimney vent, and the dirt roof was colored with flowers. Behind the storm cellar were several rows of fruit trees, some still with blossoms, others already bearing fruit. It was the kind of place that told of the presence of a woman and probably children. A family that took pride in their home that showed with everything well-built and nothing in disrepair.

They rode into the ranch yard and were greeted by a man that sat in a rocking chair on the covered porch, "Afternoon, gents. What brings you out thisaway?"

They rode closer. Eli leaned on his pommel and looked at the man with curly hair, a full beard and moustache, and a pipe with a curl of smoke rising from the bowl in his hand. He also had a Henry rifle close at hand, leaning against the log wall behind him. Eli took it all in and said, "Nice place you have here, mister. Mighty nice."

"Thank you, and?" He questioned.

"We're on the trail of four men, came through the valley yonder, by the river, yesterday afternoon. Also had a horse with two girls."

"What for you wantin' them?"

"They hit some wagons back where the road crosses the river, killed two men, wounded others, and stole the girls. The gang are all Mexican, deadly bunch."

The rancher frowned, looked at Candy, and back to Eli. "Didn't see 'em yestiddy but seen 'em afore. They was five of 'em. They be trouble."

"There were five, Candy here traded bullets with one and took a bullet himself. But the other'n was killed," stated Eli, looking from the rancher to Candy and back again. "My name is Eli McCain. This is Candalario Navarro." He paused, looking at the man, added, "Their trail was headin' up the river, movin' like they had some place in mind. Any place up that way you know about that they might be hidin' out?"

The man rocked in his chair, looking at the two before him, "My name is Nelson Eddy. This is my place. Came here in '54, built it ourselves, me'n the wife, Olive, still buildin' on it. Prob'ly won't never be done. Know these hills like I know my own hand," he jammed the pipe in his mouth, rocked forward and with elbows on his knees and hands outstretched, palms up, "and if'n they follow the river, there's a shoulder with a clearing and a log cabin sittin' back in the trees. Ain't much, but there's a stove, a table, some supplies, an' four bunks. There's a corral behind it where they could put their horses."

Eli looked at Candy, back to Nelson, "Could we get up close without bein' seen?"

"You could, longs you know its there. You'll have to climb the mountain a little, circle roun' back, ain't no windows on the back side, but there is a chimney. Onliest window is on the front, by the door."

Eli looked at Candy, grinned, and sat up in the saddle. He nodded to Nelson Eddy and started to rein around and leave, but was stopped by, "Now, hol' on there. Step down an' have some vittles. Ma's been fixin' since we saw you ridin' by the river. Figgered you'd end up here." He saw Eli's hesitation and added, "You got time to go up there an' get yourself kilt 'fore dark, don't fret none about it."

Eli grinned, glanced at Candy, and they both swung down, slapped the reins of their mounts and the lead from the packhorse around the hitch rail. Nelson said, "Thar's a wash basin roun' the side, yonder," pointing with his pipe.

"Them people in them wagons plannin' on settlin' 'round here?" asked Nelson, sitting at the head of the table and handing the plate of rolls to the visitors.

Eli grinned, "They weren't, they were goin' down

towards San Francisco or thereabouts. They're builders, gonna raise buildings, horses, and kids. But...now that two of 'em were killed, dunno. Haven't really talked about it since."

"This area's growin'. Little bit of a settlement base o' the mountain. Used to call it Strawberry Valley, now it's called Berryvale. Ol' Ross McCloud an' his wife built 'em a toll bridge cros' the Sacramento River, then built him a lumber mill. Justin Sisson built him a hotel, an' the McCloud's built 'em a resort there by them Soda Springs. It's growin' alright. Long's there's people, they need to eat, an' I'm raisin' good beef cattle," he chuckled, spooning some gravy on his potatoes.

He paused, frowning and looked at Eli, "Now if'n you was to rid us o' them varmints up at the cabin, you'd be doin' the whole community an almighty big favor, yessiree."

———

IT WAS mid-afternoon when they rode from the Eddy ranch. Nelson had given them clear directions to the different trails and the best way to approach the cabin unseen. "Now, mind you, don't neither one of us even know they're in there, but..." he shrugged as he stepped off the porch and looked up at the mountain. He shaded his eyes, pointed to the mountain, "That shoulder there, the cabin lays just o'er the rise, tucked into the trees, but you can see it by the clearing and the corner of the corral that runs down to the river, course it ain't but a crick that far up, but you know what I mean."

Nelson climbed the few stairs back to the porch, turned around, leaned on the railing post, and watched as the men mounted up. He lifted his head and said,

"Me'n the missus'll be prayin' for you—you're gonna need it!"

"Thank you, Mr. Eddy, that will be greatly appreciated!" answered Eli as he reined around and started to the gate at the edge of the ranch yard. He turned and waved at Nelson, who still stood leaning against the post on the porch. He glanced at Candy, "Looks like we got our work cut out for us, but I feel better about it now that we know where we're goin' and what we might be up against."

CHAPTER 28

AMBUSH

"He said we'd take this trail up the west-east edge of the alluvial wash, and it'd turn to cross the face of the lap of the mountain, just above the granite flats o'er thataway," declared Eli as they sat on the slight knob of the trail that offered a break in the towering pines around them. He glanced at Candy, "I reckon we're on the right trail, ya 'think?"

"Si, it is as he described. He said the cabin was at the base of that big shoulder, a little clearing that sided the headwaters of the Shasta River. Didn't he say the trapper that built it covered all these creeks, run-offs, and the little ponds or lakes on this whole mountain?"

"Yup, sounds like a long winter's hard work if you ask me."

"Si, but those old-timers talk about 'the good ol' days,'" he chuckled, shaking his head.

"Ain't my idea of making a living, tromping through snow up to your chest, just to get a beaver out of a trap, uh-uhn," he laughed as he nudged Rusty to keep moving.

The three horses moved silently through the thick

timber, ponderosa, sugar pine, sitka, spruce, fir, and even a few mountain mahogany, all added their castoff needles, cones, and snow-broken branches to the seldom-used trail, but it had been well-worn by eons of use by native hunters and more. The trail was well-carpeted, and the pine needles and aspen leaves quieted the footfalls of the horses. Lobo was scouting out front and would occasionally return to check on the travelers or sit down in the middle of the trail and wait until they came near.

The trail across the face of the mountain sided the steep mountain just above where the terrain stretched out at the edge of the alluvial plain. Eli knew they were nearing their destination and slowed the pace of the horses, stopping often to listen for any disturbance. He paused, listening, glanced back to Candy, and said in a low voice, "I hear the creek. That'd be the headwaters of the Shasta which would put us nearing the cabin. Nelson said we'd be above and behind it." He turned around in his saddle, craning back and forth trying to see through the timber, frowned, and swung his leg over the cantle to step down. He moved to the trees, leaned against a towering spruce, and searched. He paused, frowning, and watched. "There! Smoke!" He turned back to Candy, "Spotted it. We can keep going, maybe stop at the creek and tether the horses. The sun's making shadows of the mountains, paintin' the sky gold, and it'll be dark right soon. But I'd prefer to get near 'fore total dark. Then we can decide what we'll be doin'."

Candy nodded, watched Eli swing aboard the big clay-bank, and they started off on the trail, moving easy and as quiet as possible. Lobo stayed near, sensing something was happening. Within moments, they clearly heard the cascades of the creek, splashing down the steeper hillside, hurrying on its way to the bottoms. The timber had thinned somewhat, and they loosely tethered the horses, ordered Lobo to stay with the horses, and watched as he bellied down, lowering his muzzle to his paws, looking like he was in trouble. But Eli knew if the horses smelled wolf, they would be alarmed and give them away. Eli ran his fingers through Lobo's scruff, grinned, nodded to Candy. The men slipped their rifles from the scabbards, checked each weapon for loads and readiness, and started through the timber toward the cabin.

Working their way down the steep face and through the thick timber, deadfall often hindered, until, as they were climbing over a more recent deadfall, Eli spotted something that gave him an idea. He hissed at Candy to wait, and he peeled off a big chunk of bark from the downed ponderosa. He grinned as he saw the soft underbelly of the bark, chuckled as he looked up at Candy, and caught up with him. He looked at Candy, then down to the bark, "Know what I'm thinkin'?"

Candy looked and frowned, "You want to sit on it and slide down?" he asked, confused and disbelieving.

"No, that'd be stupid wouldn't it? Fun maybe, but stupid!" he chuckled quietly, "The chimney..." he stated.

Candy's eyebrows lifted, and wide-eyed, he grinned, "Si!"

They were still about forty yards above the cabin when they stopped, sat down, and looked at everything. The corrals were more to the side toward the river than behind the cabin, which would make their plan easier, but they counted only four horses in the corral. Eli looked at Candy, "One might be gone, we need to keep an eye out behind us at all times. If that one comes back too soon..." he shrugged.

Dusk had settled over the mountains, the long

shadows from the mountain range and the tall timber allowed little light, but the men's vision had slowly become accustomed to the lesser light, and at a nod from Eli, they started to move. Candy to the back of the cabin and around the far side, Eli through the corrals and along the near side of the cabin. If things went right, they would both be at the front when the men were forced out. Eli muttered a silent prayer as he went to the rail fence, whispering and talking softly to the horses. Two came near, and he stroked their heads and necks, talking softly to them as he moved through the corral. He slipped through the rails, moved to the corner of the cabin, and quietly brought the hammer of the Winchester to full cock, knowing there was already a cartridge in the chamber ready to fire.

Eli heard muffled voices from within and the sobbing of a girl. He gritted his teeth to stay his anger but breathed deep and said another prayer. A "psst" came from the far side, and Eli leaned around enough to see the hand of Candy, then his face grinning as he nodded. Movement, coughing, and stumbling could be heard from within, grumbles and curses sounded, and the door crashed open as the men came stumbling out. They stopped, leaning over, their hands on their knees as they coughed and spat. Eli saw three men, the girls apparently were bound inside, but the smoke would do them little harm.

Eli hollered, "Reach for the sky!" and his command was followed by Candy's, *"¡No se mueva!"* or, in English, "Don't move!"

The three men spun around, each man reaching for his sidearm, but Eli's Winchester roared and spat fire in the darkness, stabbing the night with lead and taking down the nearest man. He jacked another round, heard

Candy's rifle bark, and saw the men still grabbing for weapons, shouting to one another, and trying to move away. Eli shouted, "Stay where you are!" but they still moved. In the glow of light from the cabin, Eli saw the flash of light on metal and recognized it as the rising barrel of a pistol and sent a bullet with a blast from the Yellow Boy rifle that took the outlaw in the chest, driving him back a step and a stumble to fall on his back.

Candy shouted, "*¡Déjalo caer!*" and the one man still standing dropped his pistol and stood with hands raised high. Even in the dim light, it was easy to see the man's glare of anger as he glanced at the two bodies that lay at his side. Candy looked toward Eli, back to the man, but the man was grabbing behind his neck, and the flash of metal told Candy he had grabbed a knife. Candy fired, the bullet driving through the man's throat to exit the back of his neck, almost decapitating him, but wide-eyed, he crumpled to the ground. Candy glanced at Eli, back to the dead men, and with a nod to one another, they carefully approached the open door.

Candy shouted in Spanish, "*¡Sal ahora!*" and, in English, "Come out now!"

Eli heard sobs and a whimper, and he carefully leaned around the door jamb and looked into the smoky interior to see the girls, bound and gagged, back to back, on the floor. Their eyes were full of terror and tears. Eli, seeing the cabin was empty, told Candy, "Get that bark off the chimney! I'll see to the girls."

The girls were visibly excited when they recognized Eli. He quickly undid their bonds, and both girls gave him a big hug, profuse in their thanks that were intermixed with sobs and tears of relief. Asta, the older sister, asked, "Are they gone—all of them?"

"Well, three of them are, but we don't know about

the other one," began Eli, helping the girls to their feet as they went to the door to get some fresh air.

Asta nodded and said, "He left! They had a big argument, I don't know what all was said, I don't understand much Spanish and that's all they talked. But they were talking about us, I could tell. They kept pointing and looking at us. I think they were fighting about taking us back, the one man, the one that left they called Procopio, or something like that, kept talking about gold. You know, *oro*. I think they thought our families had more gold, and if they took us back, they could get it, but I'm not sure."

Eli noticed Asta kept looking toward the bodies, trembling and fidgety, holding her hands around her arms and turning away. She talked, but did not look at Eli. He could not tell if it was fear or shame and embarrassment. But his only thought was to get them back to the wagons. He looked at Anja, who also refused to look at anyone, staying close to her sister, and he asked, "Do you know where they put the money from the wagons?"

Asta answered, "Procopio took some when he left, but the rest is in the box, on the table." Eli glanced at Candy, motioned him to come close, and said, "You keep these two under your arm, I'm gonna get the money, and then we'll head back to the wagons."

"What about them?" asked Candy, motioning to the three bodies. He had dragged them near the bushes just to get them away from the cabin and the girls, "I think we should bury them."

"Yeah, you're right. You take the girls back inside, I'll go—" but stopped when Candy shook his head and said, "There's a drop-off yonder, I think we can kind of cave it in over their bodies and that'll do it."

"Take the girls inside, stay with 'em just in case the

other'n comes back. I'll get started with them," he nodded toward the bodies.

The moon was up, and the sky was clear, offering ample light for the travelers. Candy had saddled up two of the outlaws' horses, turned the others loose, and now the girls rode between the men, single file, returning on the same trail that kept to the trees. They traveled in silence, listening to the usual sounds of the night. A big owl asked his relentless questions, a pair of coyotes sang their chorus of courting, and somewhere a lone wolf bayed at the moon, making Lobo stop and listen, look back at Eli, and continue on the trail at the head of his own pack.

CHAPTER 29

REUNION

They rode into the camp of the wagons by the grey light of early morning. No one stirred, no one was on watch, the horses stood three-legged, heads hanging, until the riders pushed through the brush corral and dropped to the ground. Eli helped the girls down and spoke in whispers when he said, "Use these blankets," nodding to those he and Candy were removing from the horses, "and make your beds under the wagons. Be quiet about it and try not to wake anyone."

The girls nodded, smiling with sleepy faces, and wandered to the nearest wagon, spread the blankets and were asleep before Eli and Candy finished stripping the gear from the horses. Eli grinned at Candy, "You go on and try to get some sleep. I'm gonna start a cookfire and make some coffee." Candy nodded, chuckling and walked to the nearest wagon, dropped to the ground beside the big wheel, leaned back, pushed his hat over his eyes, crossed his arms on his chest, and was asleep before Eli had the fire started.

"Eli! You're back!" declared Olivia Hansen, mother of the girls. She looked about and looked askance to Eli, who grinned and nodded in the direction of the wagon where the sleeping girls lay. Olivia's eyes grew wide and were immediately flooded with tears as she ran to Eli, arms outstretched and almost knocked him down as she threw her arms around him and sobbed on his chest, "Oh, thank you, thank you, thank you. I was so fearful and thought the worst." She stepped back and looked up at Eli, frowning, "Were they…"

"I don't think so, they wouldn't talk about it, and I didn't think it was my place to question them. They were bound and gagged when we found them, trembling and sobbing, grateful to be found, but they would not look at me or Candy and we did not ask."

Olivia stepped back, her fist at her mouth as she stifled her sobs, shook her head, and looked at Eli, "What do I do?"

"Just love them. You're the mother, so do what you do best, love them. If they need to talk, let them choose the time and place. Maybe nothing happened, they were just frightened, but…" he shrugged. "I've never been much of a parent, seldom at home, and never had to try to raise a daughter, much less two!" he chuckled, "but you'll do fine. Just appreciate having them back."

"Oh, I do, I thank you," she said, then lifted her eyes, "and I thank the Lord."

———

MOST OF THE others had risen, come to the fire, and were thrilled to hear of the girls' safe return. They agreed to keep things quiet to give them some rest, and all pitched in to fix breakfast for everyone. Erik and Marcus

—who was already getting around, although somewhat limited—sat with Eli and were joined by Candy as they had their morning coffee and began discussing the coming days. Eli said, "I know you folks were planning on going to the bigger city, start your building work and build homes and more. Was there a special reason you were bound for San Francisco?"

"No, no special reason," answered Erik. "It was talked about among the four of us, and because it was the biggest and growing, we thought it would have more opportunity for building, and the women had talked about a café, and we also talked about raising horses. More people, more demand."

"But no family or anything like that?" asked Eli.

"No, no. We know no one there," answered Marcus, his thoughts returning to the many discussions of the four families. They had spent many evenings together, talking about their dreams of a joint business and the many opportunities they hoped to find.

"I know you have talked about the Pedersen boys driving the other wagons, but it's more than just having somebody to drive. What about whenever you get to where you're going?" He nodded to Erik and Marcus, "You have four families and two men and two boys to try to support them. That won't be easy, especially when you get to the bigger city." He paused, looking at each of the men. The two Pedersen boys had joined them and fidgeted a little, "We were talking to Nelson Eddy, he helped us find the girls, he owns a nice ranch at the upper end of the valley, and he told us about how the community along the Shasta River has been growing and how the people have been helpful of one another. Now, I'm not saying this is where you need to stop, but you might want to talk it over with the ladies, especially the widow ladies, and consider something other than the city."

"But what would we do?" asked Erik, glancing at his two boys and to Marcus.

"The same thing, and more. Small, growing communities need builders too, and it would be easier to homestead a place you could farm and raise horses and kids. If you had adjoining homesteads, it would be easier to help one another and still have your own home. And being close to the town, you could still build for others, *after* you get four homes built for yourselves." He looked around the group and added, "And in a smaller community, the people could see your homes are well-built and would be more willing to have you do some building for them. Mr. Eddy did say the agents for the railroads have come through and are talking about bringing the railroad through this area, and he also said the men that built the hotel and the lodge at the Soda Springs are wanting to add on to both buildings and would probably need help building."

Erik looked at Candy, "You know about this part of the country, what do you think?"

Candy leaned forward, holding his coffee cup with both hands, elbows on his knees, "Where we are and for the next few days, we'll be in the mountains. There are some settlements, most new, usually started because of the gold rush. Some found gold, but nothing big. Further south, it opens into a big, wide, green valley along the Sacramento River. That valley goes all the way, maybe ten days ride, to Sacramento and San Francisco. That is where I live, near San Francisco Bay."

"But what about places to live?" asked Niels Pedersen, the oldest of the boys.

Candy grinned, "It is a big country and there are

many, many places. Old towns, new towns, grand valleys, mountains and more."

Erik looked at Marcus, "Well, one thing we know, we don't want to build a home right here—not enough room!" he declared, chuckling. "Mayhaps if we get moving, we can find someplace that appeals to everyone. We need to talk to the women and..." he shrugged.

———

IT WAS difficult to ride away from the graves of the two men that had been a part of the journey and were husbands and fathers of those that now took the road to disappear into the distance, perhaps never to return. They were quiet, thoughtful, and sad, each retreating into his or her own thoughts and memories. For some, it was remembrances of long friendships, for others, precious times with family. As Candy clattered past the wagons astride his big buckskin, their thoughts turned to the present and the immediate future. The families had spent some time talking about what they would do, where they would make their homes and for those without their husbands and father, how they would make their homes.

They climbed out of the valley of the Shasta River, the Siskiyou mountains behind them, the Cascade Range marching beside them and with the towering Mount Shasta as their beacon of hope, and Black Butte to guide the way, they traveled through the valley, low rolling hills framing the fertile valley. With Black Butte behind them, the road sided Big Springs Creek and kept them in the lowland of the fertile valley. There were some farms, some appearing to be recently started with small fields, but work was underway to clear more ground. The land, promising farmland with ample water, stretched to the east up the lower apron of the big mountain. Beside the road, several fences, a few buildings, and more signs of settlement showed. A larger building seemed to shake with the sounds of a big saw telling of a lumber mill. A sign stretched across the building, McCloud Lumber Mill, and two men stood talking out front, saw the coming wagons, and waved as they neared.

Eli stopped the wagons and rode to the side of Marcus Moller, who was showing the strain of handling the team and wagon and grinned, grateful for the stop. Eli nodded toward the mill, "That's the lumber mill of McCloud, the one Nelson Eddy told me about, and that's the same McCloud that built a toll bridge across the Sacramento a bit further downstream." Eli looked around, "Looks to be plenty of land hereabouts, and it looks fertile too!" stated Eli, looking across the creek and back to the east toward Mount Shasta.

"Ja, Ja, it looks like good land. But I don't see many people," replied Marcus.

Erik Pedersen walked up beside the wagon and motioned to the lumber mill, "That the one you told about?"

"It is, and it looks like one of those men is coming this way," observed Eli.

As the man approached, he lifted his hand in greeting, "Howdy folks! Passin' through or lookin' to settle?"

Eli grinned, "I'm passin' through. They," nodding to the men and others, "aren't sure. Maybe settle, dependin'…"

The man grinned, "I'm Ross McCloud, that's my mill. We been here more'n ten years and we think it's the best place to be, growin' too!" He looked at Erik and Marcus, "Farmers?"

Erik grinned, "Not so much. We're builders..." and the conversation began as Marcus climbed down and cheerfully joined the discussion. Eli trotted back to the other wagons to explain the delay, encouraged the women to join the conversation if they were interested, and went to Candy who was sitting beside the tail-gate of the Hansen wagon, talking to the two older girls, Asta Hansen and Emilie Lund. Eli chuckled, moved past to the Lund wagon and talked with Freja, who sat beside Olivia Hansen. Olivia had turned over her wagon for Niels Pedersen to drive and chose to sit with Freja as the two widows needed the time to talk.

As Eli approached, the women looked up and forced a bit of a grin and Olivia asked Eli, "If our group were to stay here or somewhere along the way, will you stay a while with us? You know, to get us settled and safe."

"Olivia, no matter where you stop, you and the rest will be very safe. I know you're not going to stop out in the middle of nowhere, but somewhere there are plenty of neighbors and others to watch out for each other. I've never known two stronger women and with the others nearby, you'll be fine."

"I know, I was just thinking selfishly. I know you need to be looking for your sons, and I hope you find them soon. You've been so helpful, we couldn't have made it this far without you," declared Olivia, with Freja at her side nodding her agreement.

"Ladies, if I thought you and yours would not be safe, I would not leave, and I will not until you find the place you want to make your home." He grinned, removed his hat and wiped his brow, prompting Olivia to look at his wound. He looked around, "Beautiful country, don't you think?"

Freja looked around as they had already done, "Yes,

but there's not too many people or homes."

"They're further on. Most of the town, Berryville, such as it is, is a little further on and there's more down the valley. I've heard tell there are some Soda Springs that are quite refreshing, where there is a hotel and more, and a beautiful waterfall called Mossbrae Falls, and I think the folks here would like to see you become a part of the community," explained Eli. "The stage line runs through here, all the way from Sacramento north to Portland, and brings folks here, and there were some gold diggings somewhere near."

Eli heard a shout from the lead wagon, tipped his hat to the ladies, reined around, and rode to the front. As Marcus climbed aboard, Erik returned to his wagon, and Ross McCloud said, "They're going to camp down near the creek," he pointed, "I'll come down and take the folks around to see the town and more."

Eli grinned, "Sounds good. I'll help 'em make camp and see you in a short while."

———

ELI, Candy, and the youngsters stayed in camp while the ladies, men, and the older boys went in the lumber wagon with McCloud for the tour of the area. The older girls had been given instructions about getting supper started, and Eli and Candy were tasked with tending to the horses. The wagons had been pulled in a horseshoe shape with a bend in the creek and brush blocking off the end and allowing room for the animals and ample graze for them all. Eli stretched a rope across to keep the horses away from the cookfires and sleeping area. Candy had taken the younger boys, Harald Hansen, Olaf Lund, and Soren and Tobias Moller, to fetch firewood and was returning at the head of the band, empty-handed, but leading the loaded-down boys.

As they rode in the wagon, everyone could hear Ross McCloud as he told about the area, the original gold strikes, the many gold-seekers passing through, the coming of the stage line, and the promise of a soon-coming railroad. The signs of growth were there as new cabins and homes, a couple businesses, an emporium, and a tavern all had new lumber for siding and more, and Ross was enthusiastic with his answers. At the end of the tour, he took a roundabout way to return and stopped on a stretch of grassy land that lay between the townsite and his lumber mill. He stood and turned to face the others, pointing to the land, "I staked out this land shortly after we came here. I intended to make a big ranch hereabouts but just got busy with business. There's four hundred eighty acres there, and if you folks would like, I'll sell it to you at a good price. We would like to see you folks become a part of our community. We need good men," he looked at Erik, Marcus, and the Pedersen brothers, "and families. I can tell you ladies are well educated, and we need a school teacher and a good café. There's room to build your homes and raise your horses and your children. And you men that are builders, we need you."

The interest and excitement showed on the faces of most of the group, but concerns and questions would need to be resolved. Marcus looked at the others, saw their interest, and turned to McCloud, "Sir, we are very interested, but we will need some time to talk it over. We have four families, and all will be included. We started this journey together, and we decide together. So, if you will allow us, we would like to talk it over and give you an answer in the morning."

CHAPTER 30

SEPARATION

B oth men twisted around in their saddles to wave goodbye to the gathered families. The families had decided to make this area their home and the offered property would allow them to do everything they planned and do it all together, the fatherless families included. Eli glanced at Candy, surprised he had not taken more interest in the girls, but he showed no emotion at parting, and it was not Eli's way to interfere in the love lives of young people.

They crossed the Sacramento River, staying with the road that sided the river through the long Sacramento Canyon. Eli had always been a student of nature and the handiwork of God's creation, and he marveled at the meandering river where eons ago, it had cut its way through the Trinity Mountains and the foothills of the Cascade Range.

The trail took a big dogleg bend to the south and brought the travelers before Mossbrae Falls, a unique phenomenon of spring-fed water that cascaded from thickets of moss and greenery to drop into the river.

Unlike a usual waterfall that dropped over shear cliffs of solid rock, the water seemed to spring from the overhanging greenery as if the plants themselves were pouring out the water. The two men stopped and took in the marvel, sitting silently as they watched the display before them. Eli commented, "Sometimes I think God just gets a kick out of doing something different every now and then."

Candy chuckled, "It sure is different. Ain't never seen the like."

They nudged their horses on, keeping to the Siskiyou Trail, occasionally moving aside for a stagecoach but seldom meeting anyone on their way. The Sacramento River Canyon road meandered about as it followed the river through the narrows with the heavily timbered mountains pushing in and forcing the river to twist and turn to make its way south. The jagged castle crags towered over the first few miles, their ragged shoulders scratching at the blue of the sky, but as they passed the confluence of Castle Creek and the Sacramento, the crags hid behind the nearer mountains. Three more days brought them out of the mountains to break into the northernmost Sacramento Valley.

After camping one night in Poverty Flats, they took to the road that was easy traveling across the wide-open Sacramento Valley. Candy looked at Eli, "I know this area, and we're a good day's ride from Red Bluff. If you're of a mind, we could get a room in a hotel, maybe a hot bath, eat at a café, you know, pretend we're civilized like the rest of 'em."

Eli frowned, "Us, civilized? Surely not!" he chuckled and shook his head, "You know, all but the civilized part of that sounds pretty good."

Candy grinned, laughed, "Then let's pick up the pace!"

They passed several farms, many with fruit orchards and wide fields of grains, one with the beginnings of a vineyard. The road widened and had seen considerable wagon traffic. The men moved aside for a long line of freighters bound to the north country, followed by a long pack train of probably fifty-plus heavily loaded mules. They passed a pair of farm wagons loaded to the brim with crates of vegetables and fruits, moved over for a passing stagecoach, and marveled at the number of people on a road that seemed to be in the middle of farm country.

It was dusk when they rode into the burgeoning town of Red Bluff. They passed a flour mill, a lumber mill, and a fruit-packing barn and started down the main road. They passed the county building with the sheriff's office and jail, the courthouse, spotted a livery with a hotel across the way, and nodded to one another, grinning at the prospect of a pleasant evening.

The hotel did not offer baths, but there was a Chinese laundry and bath house next door, and the men took advantage of the business. Just down the street from the Tremont Hotel was a café called the Bread Board Chop House, and the men took the last table that was tucked in a back corner but afforded a view of the entire dining room. When the young woman came to the table, coffee pot in hand and a smile on her face, Candy returned her smile and leaned back to look at her as she poured their cups full. *"Buenas Noches, Señorita,"* Candy greeted, smiling broadly. His sombrero hung on the chair, and he had brushed his bolero and put on a clean white shirt with a string tie. He presented a handsome picture and his broad smile and laughing eyes always attracted the ladies.

The woman blushed, dropped her eyes, and asked, "And what would you gentlemen like for your meal?"

They ordered, and Candy grinned, hoping to see the young woman again, but she disappeared into the kitchen and did not show herself after that. When they finished their meal and stood to leave, Eli noticed a table of men with a look of roughness about them that were watching him and Candy. Eli turned his back to them, nudged Candy to leave, and the two left the café. When they stepped onto the boardwalk, Eli asked, "Did you see those three men at the table near the window?"

Candy frowned, "No, why?"

"They were watching us, you especially, when you talked with the waitress. They did not look too happy about it."

"Eh, so? What can they do? I did nothing wrong."

Darkness had fallen, and several windows were laying gold rectangles of light on the boardwalk as the men walked down the way. The sound of a tin-panny piano came from a building across the street that had a sign, *Bluffs Dance Hall and Tavern*. Candy nudged Eli, "Let's go there. Maybe meet some ladies, dance a little, eh?" he laughed as he started to cross the street. Eli begrudgingly followed, he was not interested in meeting any ladies or dancing, but he stayed with Candy, if for no other reason than to keep him out of trouble.

When they entered, the piano player was being replaced with a group of musicians that held instruments, including a fiddle, a concertina, a jews harp, a harmonica and a guitar. As they began playing *Camptown Races*, the tables emptied and the dance floor filled. Eli and Candy stood at the long bar that had a big mirrored back bar and two bartenders. "You men drinkin' or dancin'?" growled the nearest bartender.

They looked at the man, then Candy looked at the girls on the dance floor and the few that were seated along the edge of the floor, their backs against the wall, and Candy replied, "Dancing and Drinking!" he declared, grinning. He looked at Eli, who responded, "I'll watch for a while first."

"Tickets are a dollar for ten, and drinks start at a quarter!"

Candy dug a dollar from his pocket, plunked it on the bar, and the bartender grinned as he rolled off a string of tickets. "Any of 'em'll do!" growled the barkeep, nodding to the girls.

Eli flipped a quarter to the man, "Cold beer."

When the band finished *Camptown*, they gave a short pause for the girls to return to their seats, then started off with *Listen to the Mocking Bird*. Candy walked quickly to the row of seated ladies, smiled, and grinned as he gave a slight bow and asked a raven-haired beauty for a dance. She smiled, held her hand out, and when Candy started to take her hand, she shook her head, and he gave her a ticket. She tucked the ticket into her bosom, stood with a smile, and off they went to the dance floor.

The bartender placed a mug of beer with an overflowing head of foam before Eli and Eli turned to watch the dancers. Eli sipped the beer and watched the dancers, especially Candy and his partner, as they whirled around the dancefloor, Candy showing his steps and impressing not only the woman he was with but others that watched. The band changed the tempo with their next song, *Jeanie with the Light Brown Hair*. Candy gave his partner another ticket and led her back to the dance floor. He held her close, and she seemed to enjoy his dancing and smiled all the while. As the song slowed and was nearing the end, a bull of a man stormed through the dancers, growling and pushing others aside. Eli recognized him as one of the men in the café that had been watching both men as they left, and now he could tell the man was heading directly for Candy, who appeared to be oblivious to the interruption.

The bull grabbed Candy's shoulder, pulled him away from the woman, and spun him around, growling, "Stay away from my woman!" Candy staggered a moment and heard the woman cry, "Bull, not again!" she pleaded. Candy looked at the man, and whatever was said was unheard by most as the band was finishing the music. The bull grabbed Candy's sleeve, cocked his arm, and as he swung, Candy stepped back and jerked his arm free. The fist flew by his face, but Candy brought a stiff arm left to the bully's face, and when he flinched aside, Candy brought his right from the floor and buried it in the man's gut, bending him over where Candy brought up his knee and splattered the big man's nose across his face.

The bull roared, came erect, and spread his arms wide, eyes showing whites and nostrils flaring as he growled, "I'm gonna kill you fer that!" and charged with a roar that rivaled that of a grizzly with a toothache. Candy grinned, feinted to the man's left, spun around, and brought his elbow against the man's face and neck, driving him to the side, stumbling over two other dancers.

Eli watched, saw movement near the door, and recognized the other two men that had sat at the table with the bully. They started pushing their way through the crowd, and Eli shook his head, mumbled, "Not how I wanted to spend this night!" and started after the two.

As Candy stepped back to allow Bull to get up, the other two grabbed him from behind, one man on each arm, and held him.

Bull growled, "Now you're gonna git what's comin'!" and stood before Candy, blood running from his nose and ear. He wiped at it, saw the blood on his hand and his eyes flared. He brought his arm back to ready his punch, but Eli was behind him. Eli grabbed the man's arm, pulled him off balance, and spun him to the side. Eli stepped close, grabbed the man's bloody beard, drove his hip into the man's side, jerked on the beard, and rolled him over his hip to drop him face-first to the hard floor. The thud of his weight reverberated through the dance hall. Several of the dancers, who now stood watching, winced and groaned at the impact.

Candy kicked his feet out, dropped to his haunches, and dragged the men down with him. They lost their grip on his arms. Candy came to his feet, turned, and drove a left jab into the mouth of the nearest man, grabbed the other by his shirt and slapped him, back-handed him and slapped him again, then drove a jab straight into his nose, splattering it across his face and splashing blood over his chest and shoulders.

Candy glanced at Eli, but suddenly the dance had turned into a brawl as men joined in the melee. Fists were flying, men were shouting, women screaming, and pandemonium ruled. Eli saw a man driven back onto a table that crashed to the floor, and a chair was smashed down to drive him into the splintered table top. When the three assailants tried to get back to Eli and Candy, who stood back to back, watching, the three were suddenly in the middle of the melee and had others to fight. When two women began ripping at clothes and pulling each other's hair, Eli said, "Let's get outta here while we still can."

With a chuckle, Candy said, "Lead the way!" and followed as Eli parted the bodies of the men and women that paid little attention to anyone other than whoever they were fighting. After ducking a few punches and shoving a couple aside, they finally made it to the door and pushed through the gathered onlookers, laughing as they stepped into the dark street. "So much for a nice peaceful, restful night," drawled a laughing Candy, his hand on Eli's shoulder as they walked to the hotel.

CHAPTER 31

VALLEJO

The sun was peeking over the eastern hills and painting the bellies of the dark clouds with brilliant reds when Eli and Candy rode from the town of Red Bluff. The trail sided the Sacramento River and when Eli twisted around in his saddle, he saw two paddle wheel steamships tied off at the wharf below the town. The bluffs that gave the town its name rose from the river with red dirt bluffs scattered with willows and manzanita and stretched to the east. The trail before them was long, well-traveled, and sided the Sacramento River, although often well away from the winding stream, and they expected a hot day of travel.

The sun was nearing its zenith, and the sky was void of clouds. The men had shed jackets and scarves and unbuttoned their shirts, all in an attempt to get some air on a day where there was no breeze to provide relief from the scorching sun. A small creek with but a trickle of water crossed their trail and made its way to the bigger river, but the men saw shade trees that promised some relief. The horses showed lather under the blankets, at the cinch, and under the martingales, and they, too, paused when they came to the shade. The men slid down, led the horses to water, stripped the gear to let them roll, rubbed them down with some dry grass, and picketed them to graze in the shade.

They had no desire for hot coffee, and after dousing their heads in the creek and splashing water on their chests and necks, Eli and Candy retreated to the cool shade. With a handful of jerky and some freshly picked manzanita berries, they were determined to get some rest and wait till the cool of the evening to continue their journey.

Eli chose a pale barked sycamore, stretched out on the bed of leaves, and with his saddle for a pillow, his hat over his eyes, and Lobo at his side, he was soon asleep. Always the cautious one, Eli had lain the Colt shotgun beside his leg, taken the thong from the Colt in the holster at his hip, and adjusted his position to make himself comfortable without removing the LeMat at his back. Although some might think it uncomfortable to sleep with all the weapons, it was in its own way, comforting.

Candy picked a buckeye that grew in the shadow of the sycamore but had lower branches and a thicker carpet of leaves that beckoned the hot and tired Candy. They were near enough to hear the chuckle and gurgle of the bigger river, mixed with the giggle of the little stream nearby, and it was just enough to lull them to a peaceful sleep.

Eli was brought awake by the low growl of Lobo, and he opened his eyes just enough to peer out from under the brim of his hat and saw booted feet slowly approaching. His right arm and leg hid the shotgun, and he grasped the grip without showing any movement. He grunted, whispered to Lobo, "Easy boy," and moved as if changing position without waking and drew up one knee, then lay still as if he had dropped off to sleep again, but he watched the boots that were about ten feet away. He heard the hissing whisper of the booted man, "Get their guns, quick!" That told Eli there were others, but he could not tell how many.

He felt Lobo moving, readying to attack, and Eli lunged to his feet, both hands on the shotgun as he cocked the hammer and brought the weapon to bear on the booted man before him, the move startling the intruder and freezing him as he looked at the big barrel of the shotgun. Lobo launched himself at a man off to Eli's right, and Candy stopped the other when he cocked the hammer and said, "No, no, señor!" and came to his feet.

Lobo's lunge with teeth bared, eyes blazing orange, and his full weight startled the man and drove him to his back with Lobo astraddle of his chest, jaws snapping and fangs reaching for his throat. The man screamed, kicked, and shot his pistol into the air until Eli ordered, "Back, Lobo!" And the black wolf lifted his head, still growling, lips curled off his fangs, and still atop the man. Eli, with the shotgun leveled at the booted man, called out, "Best not move less'n you want to have your throat ripped out!"

Eli looked at the booted man and recognized him as the one called Bull that started the fight in the dance hall. "Hey, Candy, recognize these three?"

"Si, they are the ones that wanted to dance with us at the hall!" he chuckled. "But they din't know how!" he laughed. Candy sidestepped a little closer to Eli and motioned the man under his gun to move closer to Bull, who was glaring and grumbling after Eli made him drop his pistol. The man under Candy's gun had also been unarmed and now stood beside his partner.

"So, how're we gonna teach these fellas to dance?" chuckled Eli. "Should we show them how to lift their feet?"

"You mean like this?" asked Candy and fired off two rounds at the feet of the men, which made the lift their boots in shock.

Bull glared at the two, growling, "I'm gonna kill you both fer this!"

Candy laughed, "I think you said that before, Bull, but look at us now. We're all just dancing under the trees!" he laughed, and fired another round at Bull's feet, making him stagger back and kick at the dirt, fearful of another close shot from Candy.

Eli glanced around, saw the three horses of the men tethered to the brush near the creek about thirty yards away, and looked at Candy, "Maybe we could convince them they are not cut out for dancing. What do you think?"

"That would be good, but how?" asked Candy, laughing again.

"Go get their horses, bring 'em here. I'll keep these three waiting for the next dance." He looked at the two together and called out to the wolf, "Lobo! Come here," He waited until he saw movement from the black wolf and said to the man, "You, don't try anything. Leave your pistol where it is and come over here!"

Eli looked at the others, "And since this is a ten gauge shotgun, you don't want me shooting at your feet to help your dance step!"

Bull's face fell as his expression of anger seemed to melt when he realized that Eli held a shotgun. Every man knew a shotgun's blast could spread as much as three feet in a distance of ten or more feet, and each ball of the double-aught buckshot was almost as big as the slug of a pistol and would tear a man to pieces. Bull said, "Be careful with that thing, it could kill us all!"

Eli chuckled, "That's the idea, and right now, I just can't think of any reason *not* to kill you all!"

Candy returned with the horses, and Eli nodded and looked at the three, "Now, take off your boots and your britches!"

"Do what?" asked an incredulous Bull.

"You heard me, now!" declared Eli, lifting the shotgun and firing a round over their heads, which made them duck, drop to their haunches, and start stripping off their boots and britches. "Socks too, and toss 'em all to Candy!" ordered Eli, and the men complied. Eli chuckled to see the men, two with the typical union suits, one without anything except the long tail of his linen shirt, which did little toward modesty.

"Candy, put all their stuff on the horses, pistol belts and pistols included, tie the boots together, and hang them over the pommels." Eli grinned and ordered the men to lay down on their bellies, turn to face the creek, and not move. When Candy came close, "You keep them here. I'll start saddling my horse and the pack horse, then you can saddle up, and we'll leave."

Candy frowned, "What about them?"

Eli chuckled, "You'll see…"

————

ELI AND CANDY sat astride their horses, Eli holding the lead of one of the men's horses, Candy with two. The grey pack horse often followed free rein, and Lobo stood beside Rusty, hackles raised and growling at the men. Eli still held the shotgun on the men, "Now, fellas, you just haven't been able to learn the dance steps, so maybe this will help you. We'll take your horses up the trail a ways, cut 'em loose, and run 'em up the road back toward Red Bluff. Now, if you're smart, which I don't think you are, but if so, you'll do your best to catch up to your horses and put your clothes on and go back to town and forget all about us. If we see you again, there'll be no dancing, no talking, we'll just shoot to kill!"

Anger flared in the men's eyes, but when Eli said they would shoot to kill, their expression changed, and when Candy fired another shot at their feet to make them dance another jig, anger turned to fear. Eli shook his head, slapped legs to Rusty, and the two men and six horses kicked up a cloud of dust as they took back to the road. They did not turn toward Red Bluff but went south. At the next confluence of a creek and the river, Eli started to the river and splashed into the stream to cross over. The bluffs were close to the river, and once across, they slapped the rumps of the horses and drove them into the woods at the base of the bluffs. He looked at Candy, "They'll want to stay in the shade, and it'll be a while before those outlaws find 'em. By then, we'll be long gone!"

They established a pattern of traveling six hours from first light, resting five or six hours in the heat of the afternoon, and traveling another five or six hours during the cool of dusk and early night. Six days of continuous travel across the flats of farmland and rolling hills brought them into the bustling town of Vallejo that lay across the Napa River from the Mare Island Naval Shipyard, the first U.S. Navy base on the Pacific Ocean. The big moon bounced its pale golden lances off the water as the men rode down Georgia Street to the livery. Candy nodded to the Vallejo Livery, "We'll leave our horses here. There's a hotel just down the street."

"We're getting close to your home, aren't we?" asked Eli.

"Si, from here, we will take a ferry across the Carquinez strait, and it is maybe a half-day ride."

They were both tired, as were the horses, and it would feel good to have a hot meal and a comfortable bed to get a good night's rest. Tomorrow would see time at the rancho, then Eli planned on crossing the bay to San Francisco and, hopefully, get word about his boys.

CHAPTER 32

SAN FRANCISCO

The deepwater shipping channel that fed the town of Pacheco showed the bark *D.C. Murray* and the Australian steamer *Cyphernes* at the dock, loading and unloading. The *Murray* was taking on a load of grain, and the *Cyphernes*, after offloading its cargo of pineapple and more from Honolulu, was taking on a load of coal. Eli had not expected to see ocean-going vessels this far inland, but the deepwater channel afforded the nearby farmers and miners access to the world and gave prosperity in return.

The two men pushed past the wharf and the main street of businesses—all of whom appeared to be prospering with farm wagons, horses, buggies, and buckboards crowding the street—people milling about on the boardwalks, and horses tied off at the hitchrails. Eli looked at Candy, "Didn't expect to see this! This is a booming little town!" he declared, twisting around in his saddle to look at all the businesses. He nodded to the Hale & Brother general store and asked, "Good place to re-supply?"

"Si, they are known for good merchandise and prices. The rancho does business there," responded Candy, tipping his hat to a pair of young women that were looking his way as they twirled their parasols against the bright sun.

The town of Pacheco was on the property of the Rancho Monte del Diablo, and the buildings of the Pacheco family were adjacent to the town, built on a bit of a rise that overlooked the land and the village. Candy led the way to the courtyard of the Pacheco home and the nearby adobe houses and more. He reined up at the hitchrail before the two-story, white-washed stucco home with a portico where both levels had chairs, benches, tables, and more that showed the covered porches were often used by the family.

Candy stepped down, motioned Eli to follow, and took the steps to the porch. He paused for Eli to come alongside and started to the door, but stopped when the door opened, and the elder Pacheco stepped through, a broad smile on his face and arms wide to welcome Candy. They spoke their greetings in Spanish, but when Salvio Pacheco saw Eli, he frowned, stepped back, and extended his hand to Eli, "Pardon me, señor, we are being rude. I am Salvio Pacheco, and you are?"

Eli grinned and extended his hand to shake, "I am Elijah McCain. Candy and I have been traveling together all the way from Astoria on the Columbia."

Salvio grinned, nodding, looking from Eli to Candy, and added, "Then you will join me for lunch, and the two of you can tell me all about your journey!" He grasped Eli's arm in his right hand, Candy's in his left, and led the two men into the palatial home, through the long entryway and out the back doors to the extensive patio and covered portico, where they were seated around a table. Salvio said, "Now, begin!" and Candy began from the riverboat at Astoria and related the high points of their journey with special comments regarding the trail and the possibility of taking a herd of cattle on a drive from Pacheco to Portland.

It was mid-afternoon when the men left the table and walked through the home to let Candy go to his home and see his mother and other family. Eli said his good-byes and rode from the Rancho, twisted around in the saddle, and waved to his friend after both had promised to try to get together before Eli's search took him from the area.

Candy and Salvio had given Eli directions to make his way through the mountainous and heavily timbered country west of the Rancho, a distance of about fifteen miles that would take the rest of the day and into the dim light of dusk. But that suited Eli, for he would rather make camp in the woods, a little secluded and away from the crowds of the towns and settlements that were populating this part of California.

Having made his camp by the dim light of fading dusk, he chose a high point on a long ridge with tall ponderosa, and come first light, he rolled from his blankets, stood beneath a towering pine, and gazed at the vista of the San Francisco bay. It stretched as far to the south as the morning light and the low wispy clouds of the morning would allow him to see. To the north, it bent around the point of land and out of sight. Across the bay, he could see the mouth of the bay and, on the south edge, the rolling hills of the San Francisco peninsula. He turned back to his gear, grabbed his binoculars, and had a good look-see and was pleased when he saw at least three clipper ships, two at the wharf, one laying at anchor, and many other ships, both sailing and steamers.

He reached down, ran his fingers through Lobo's scruff, glanced at the horses, and said, "Well, fellas, here we are. Let's get a move on and get across on that ferry and see if we can find out anything about the boys!"

Salvio had encouraged Eli to take a ferry on the creek route where he would book crossing on a ship on the Oakland Estuary. When he arrived at the docks, he boarded the ferry *Contra Costa*, which had stalls for horses, and Eli stayed with his animals, keeping Lobo close. As the ferry landed and all the passengers and their animals disembarked, Eli had a look around and decided to check some of the docks, talk to some stevedores and hopefully learn something about the *Flying Cloud* and maybe the twins.

When he mounted the wharf, he saw he had a considerable task before him, but with a long look at the many ships, he spotted a clipper that caught his attention, and with a frown, he mounted Rusty and started toward the ship. He was pleased to see the three tall masts with sails furled. He imagined the magnificent sight the ship would make with all 28 jibs and sails catching wind and driving the clipper across the waves. He chuckled as he remembered his time before the mast, shook his head, and nudged Rusty toward the dock. Eli stepped down, watched the stevedores loading the big ship, saw one barking orders, and with the horses ground hitched, he walked onto the dock, approached the man, and asked, "Cap'n aboard?"

"Who's askin'?" growled the mate, keeping his eyes on the crew and others as they stowed the cargo.

"Colonel Elijah McCain of McCain Shipbuilders," stated Eli, in the voice he had often used as a commandant of calvary.

The mate turned to look at him, looked up and down,

and said, "You ain't no shipbuilder!"

"And you're not the captain! Where can I find him?" growled Eli, stepping forward and showing as much bluster as the mate.

The mate stepped back, "He ain't aboard. He's in town. You might find him at the Bon Ton, that's where he usually eats and stays when he ain't on board."

Eli nodded, glanced at the crew, looked about, and turned back to the mate, "You have any crew on board name of Paine? Two brothers, twins, Jubal and Joshua?"

The mate, Second Mate Koch, frowned, slowly shook his head, and grunted, "No one by that name on this crew!"

Eli had been watching the crew and the long-shoremen as they loaded the cargo and saw one man that appeared to be listening in on their conversation but staying clear of the mate. When the mate answered in the negative, the man stopped, shook his head, and walked to the end of the dock where the many boxes, crates, and more were waiting to be loaded. Eli looked back to the mate, "Alright. Thanks for the information," and turned to go back to the horses. He saw the lone seaman standing near the boxes and saw him motion. Eli casually caught the reins of the horses, led them out of sight of the mate, and stopped near the lone seaman. He looked at the man, "You've got something to say?"

"Were you askin' 'bout the brothers, Jubal and Joshua?"

Eli frowned, "Yes, their last name is Paine, they're twins. They're my step-sons. You see 'em?"

"Yeah, they were shanghaied in Astoria with me 'n two others. They were with us till we got to here the first time, couple weeks back. They jumped ship."

Eli grinned, "Sounds right. That's 'bout what they'd do."

"No, no, you don't understand. They met a couple sisters, they was kinda sweet on each other, and the girls wanted 'em to meet up with 'em down in Monterey. So, they jumped ship here, and the girls stayed aboard with their ma and went to Monterey."

"You know the girls' names?"

"Only that they were Gabrielle and Giséle, don't know their last names. But they was sumpin', yessir!" he grinned and chuckled at the thought.

"And your name?" asked Eli.

"Whitcomb. Those are good boys, they worked hard, learned quick, but you know love!" he chuckled again. "If you find 'em, tell 'em I said good luck!"

"I'll do that. Thanks, Whitcomb!"

Eli pulled Rusty close, swung aboard, nodded to Whitcomb, and started to the town. He asked a passerby for the location of a livery, got directions, and was soon putting the horses in stalls and stripping the gear. The smithy stood by the stalls as Eli stripped the gear, and Eli asked, "What hotel you recommend?"

"Stayin' long?" asked the smithy, leaning on the stall fence, resting his chin on his arms as he watched.

"No, not long, maybe a night or two. Somethin' good. I want to get cleaned up, have a good meal, good night's rest, you know."

"Prob'ly the Bon Ton. It's a little stiff, but folks like it. Foods good. It's down the street 'bout a block, on the right."

"Thanks, I'll give it a try. Alright if I keep my gear in the stalls?"

The smithy nodded, "Ever'body does." He paused and nodded to the wolf, "He stayin' too?"

Eli grinned, "He doesn't like gettin' too far from the horses. He'll sleep in the stall with this'n," answered Eli, finishing Rusty's rubdown.

———

When Eli walked into the dining room of the Bon Ton, he looked about, and many were looking at him. He was an impressive figure, with black pin-stripe trousers, a black cutaway jacket with a black brocade waistcoat, and a white shirt with a string tie. The slight bulge at his left waist showed his holstered Colt .44 Army pistol, but his stance, carriage, and expression spoke confidence. He strode to a table, took his seat, and looked about at the other diners. He spotted a couple he assumed to be the captain of the *Cloud* and his wife. When the waiter came to his table, Eli ordered and also ordered a bottle of wine to be delivered to the table of the captain.

He watched as the waiter did his bidding, and when the couple received the wine, they looked at him, the captain lifted his glass to Eli, and both nodded to the other. The waiter came to Eli's table and said, "The Captain and his lady invite you to join them."

"Thank you, I'll do that," replied Eli, rising from his seat and going to the table of the couple. He stopped, nodded to the woman, looked at the captain, and introduced himself, "Captain, I am Colonel Elijah McCain of McCain shipbuilders of Essex, Maryland."

The Captain stood, accepted Eli's offered hand, and said, "And I am Captain Creesy of the *Flying Cloud*, and this is my wife, Eleanor."

Eli gave a slight bow to the woman, "Pleased to meet you both, and you are the navigator, are you not?" asked

Eli, accepting the motion of the Captain and seating himself.

They talked about their common interests, ships, and the building of great vessels, and Eli turned the conversation to the current voyages of the *Flying Cloud*.

"Well, we just completed a voyage from Astoria, Oregon, carrying passengers, gold, and timber to San Francisco and Monterey. Now we're taking on flour, lumber, wine, passengers, and more as we set sail for Australia and New Zealand. Our new owner, the Black Ball Line, has begun to focus on down under," he chuckled, taking a drink of the wine sent over by Eli. He looked at Eli, "And what brings you, a shipbuilder from the Atlantic, to the coast of the Pacific?"

"I've been on an extended search. There are two men," as he spoke, he retrieved the tintype of the twins and passed it to the captain, who leaned closer to his wife as they both looked, "that I've been looking for, and I understand they were on your crew for a while."

The captain frowned and looked at Eli, "Yes! They were on my crew, and they jumped ship when we were here in San Francisco! I've been looking for them, asking around, but have not found them. I had a warrant sworn out for them as well." He gritted his teeth as he handed the tintype back to Eli, "And why do you want them? Are they outlaws of some sort?"

Eli slowly grinned, "No, they are my sons."

The captain frowned, "They said their names were Paine, and you are a McCain, are you not?"

"They are my step-sons. I was looking for them on a promise made to their mother, who died recently, and they do not know of her death." Eli grinned, noticed the sympathetic expression from the woman, and continued,

"And, Captain, I suggest you get the warrant nullified. You and I both know those men were shanghaied at the Seafeldt Corner Tavern in Astoria, and you do not have a contract with the boys. If you told the officers that you did, that could get you in trouble because any contract you have would have been forged by you. However, we'll forget about the warrant if you can tell me the names of the young ladies that were enamored with my sons and where they live. Perhaps they might tell me more about the whereabouts of my sons." Eli grinned as he lifted his coffee cup and took a long draught, waiting for the captain to respond.

It was evident by the expression and reaction of the captain that he was less than pleased with Eli's demands, but he also knew that Eli was right in what was said. The captain looked at his wife, who gave a slight nod, then looked back at Eli. "The girls are the daughters of Geneviéve Devereaux of Monterey. They are a well-known family. Mrs. Devereaux is a widow, but they are a wealthy family, and you should have no trouble finding them."

Eli grinned, slipped the napkin from his lap, placed it on the table, rose to his feet, and looked at Eleanor Creesy, "Ma'am," nodding and to the captain, "Captain. Thank you. May you have a safe voyage." He turned away and went to his room. He was pleased, he had good news about the boys. He chuckled that they were pursuing two young ladies of considerable wealth and believed that if this was real for them, they would stay in one place a little longer than usual, making the chances of his finding them greater than what he had known before.

Tomorrow he would get an early start and would begin his journey south to Monterey. With a grin, he knelt beside his bed and offered his thanks to the Lord for all He had done for him. "And, Lord, let this trip be safe, uneventful, and productive. The boys need to know about their mother, and they need to set their sights on their future. And, Lord, it would be great if I could quit chasin' 'em and maybe settle down my own self."

A Look At: Rocky Mountain Saint

The Complete Series

BESTSELLING WESTERN AUTHOR B.N. RUNDELL TAKES READERS ON A JOURNEY THROUGH THE WILDERNESS IN THIS COMPLETE MOUNTAIN MAN SAGA.

Holding on to the dream of living in the Rocky Mountains that he shared with his father, Tatum begins a journey that takes him through the lands of the Osage and Kiowa and—ultimately—to the land of the Comanche.

But the wilderness makes demands on anyone who tries to master the mountains.

Follow Tatum Saint, man of the mountains, on his journey from boyhood to manhood—where he faces everything from the wilds of the wilderness…to forces of nature and historic wars.

Rocky Mountain Saint: The Complete Series includes Journey to Jeopardy, Frontier Freedom, Wilderness Wanderin', Mountain Massacre, Timberline Trail, Pathfinder Peril, Wapiti Widow, Vengeance Valley, Renegade Rampage, Buffalo Brigade, Territory Tyranny, Winter Waifs, Mescalero Madness, and Dine' Defiance.

AVAILABLE NOW

About the Author

Born and raised in Colorado into a family of ranchers and cowboys, B.N. Rundell is the youngest of seven sons. Juggling bull riding, skiing, and high school, graduation was a launching pad for a hitch in the Army Paratroopers. After the army, he finished his college education in Springfield, MO, and together with his wife and growing family, entered the ministry as a Baptist preacher.

Together, B.N. and Dawn raised four girls that are now married and have made them proud grandparents. With many years as a successful pastor and educator, he retired from the ministry and followed in the footsteps of his entrepreneurial father and started a successful insurance agency, which is now in the hands of his trusted nephew.

He has also been a successful audiobook narrator and has recorded many books for several award-winning authors. Now realizing his life-long dream, B.N. has turned his efforts to writing a variety of books—from children's picture books and young adult adventure books, to the historical fiction and western genres, which are his first loves.

Made in the USA
Columbia, SC
20 September 2023